THE ANTIQUE DEALER'S WOMEN

on THE ANTIQUE DEALER'S WOMEN:

'The prose is so elegant, so sensuous, so assured. Wonderful writing.'

Elaine Feinstein

on DOUBLE VISION:

'Andrew Kennedy's stories are vignettes of insightful and humane understanding. They are of a concise maturity all too rare in the current climate of narrative.'

George Steiner

THE ANTIQUE DEALER'S WOMEN

Confessions

Andrew K Kennedy

*For Zen
with my best wishes
from Andrew
Cambridge, 6 Nov. 2008*

Meadows Press
CAMBRIDGE

Copyright © Andrew K Kennedy 2006
First published in 2006 by Meadows Press
5 South Green Road, Cambridge CB3 9JP

Distributed by Gazelle Book Services Limited
Hightown, White Cross Mills, South Rd, Lancaster, England LA1 4XS

The right of Andrew K Kennedy to be identified as the author of the work has been asserted herein in accordance with the Copyright, Designs and Patents Act 1988.

All rights reserved. This book is sold subject to the condition that it shall not, by way of trade or otherwise, be lent, resold, hired out or otherwise circulated without the publisher's prior consent in any form of binding or cover other than that in which it is published and without a similar condition including this condition being imposed on the subsequent purchaser.

All of the characters in this book are fictitious and any resemblance to actual people, living or dead, is purely imaginary.

British Library Cataloguing in Publication Data
A catalogue record for this book is available from the British Library.

ISBN 0-9536731-1-1
ISBN 978-0-9536731-1-7

Typeset by Amolibros, Milverton, Somerset
This book production has been managed by Amolibros
Printed and bound by T J International Ltd, Padstow, Cornwall, UK

Contents

I	Virgin	1
II	Married Woman	39
III	Divorcee	85
IV	Widow	115
V	Unmarried	145
	Epilogue	163
	Editor's Afterword	169

I

Virgin

I must confess I did not welcome a surprise encounter at that time. I had been enjoying a rare phase of monkish seclusion in this much-loved European city, with rich occasions for solitary contemplation. Never before have I been so contented in the sense of not wanting anything or anyone. After seeing hundreds of paintings in the afternoon, it was a fresh stimulus just to gaze at a living view, the magnificent townscape, letting my eyes wander over the rooftops between the red Duomo and the dark green Arno. In the clear air of early evening the whole panorama was shining as if arranged for an old master's canvas. A perfect return, after some thirty years, as if I was seeing all this for the first time – memories of youth intensified. Intoxication without anything toxic in me.

I could feel Spring coming, the evening was mellow and I was just waiting to get a twilight view of the city from the piazzale. All appetite for adventure was suspended by the spirit of the place. It was unthinkable to take any initiative (especially towards female company). Why roam the streets at night in search of encounters? I had no desire to imitate my former self. Not only was I older and more mature but, I recall thinking this at the time, I felt rejuvenated without needing a younger person's touch. A stranger might only shatter the splendour of the skyline.

An ethereal voice interrupted my meditation. Coming from nowhere, perhaps from above, from a slope I had not noticed, the voice greeted me with a lilt, in Latin: *Quid agis?* or *Quo vadis?* Summoned by an angel, over-exposed to all those images in the museum? Turning my head, I saw a strange, tall girl, bright eyes, delicate skin, with a halo around her head. She continued to address me in Latin for several minutes, until I managed to communicate that I could understand and preferred Italian. For some reason, she then switched to fluent but not faultless English. At that point she shook off her halo. The apparition, however, did not vanish when humanised: sandals neatly strapped with thin black straps over bare skin, kneeling on the grass beside my bench, retrieving a neat envelope from an elegant little leather handbag, smiling, breathing audibly. She took out a few art postcards and presented them to me, saying something solemn like 'a gift from our Christian humanist culture' in a light, far from solemn voice. Ringing in my ears, her voice dispelled the sceptic's resistance for the time being.

I nearly laughed out loud when one of the pictures turned

out to be Fra Angelico's *Annunciation*, a reproduction of the San Marco mural I had contemplated earlier in the day: the Virgin on the right of the picture seated under a round arch on a plain wooden stool, arms crossed over her breasts in full humility, flesh-coloured dress that does not suggest flesh, dark blue cloak fully covering the legs and spreading forward, bright narrow eyes in concentrated astonishment meeting the gaze of the angelic messenger – in readiness for a miraculous conception. Religious art almost persuades like nothing else. However, at the time I wanted only to normalise our encounter for the sake of simplicity, with polite exploratory phrases, when she suddenly cried out *subito*!, slipped her feet into the sandals, turned and ran from me at breakneck speed.

At sunset I felt as if abandoned by a close friend; by midnight I was tossing restlessly in bed; by the following morning I longed for her. Admittedly I thought that was folly, and I instantly accepted that any pursuit of the object (what a word!) would be hopeless, for the city was large enough for a nameless person to disappear, without trace, for all time. Any attempt to search would have turned me into a suspect – making inquiries at the police station, at the nearest college of art or wherever. I was preparing to give her up, without feeling defeated. So the following day I went for a swim quite calmly. After the swim, putting on my clothes in the changing room, I checked my pockets as I always do and found a blue envelope with three picture postcards –

my forgotten present from her. I gazed at the pictures with as much attention as I would give to an original, almost with reverence, when I noticed some words scribbled on the back of the blue envelope in tiny, barely legible handwriting. I gazed and saw, or rather slowly deciphered, as an archaeologist might break the code of an obscure inscription, a name and an address.

She was astonished when I presented myself at her door on a sunny afternoon. Astonished but accepting; at all events there was no sign of her wanting to reject my improvised initiative. Yet, within minutes of our exchanging a few formalities, she felt the need to call in her older sister who evidently lived with her in the same apartment.

'This is Carla, not only my sister but my best friend,' she said with a strange enthusiasm that she immediately extended to me, adding a fresh tone to her earlier courtesy:

'And now we can begin to be friends, if we speak the right word and do the right thing.' Again, these solemn-sounding phrases were spoken lightly, finishing off with peels of laughter.

'I'm Camilla, I don't think I told you. And you are?'

I told her my name and there was a brief silence.

'Ah, Donaldo-call-me-Don,' she seemed to mimic, cheekily adding, 'Don, Don who? Don Giovanni?'

I was embarrassed, thinking that I was already suspect in her eyes, she had x-rayed me. But it was a passing remark, a joke. Next she offered me tea in the blandest way, 'Since you come from England...'

She left the room but returned soon carrying a tray loaded with a teapot and quite ordinary porcelain cups and saucers arranged in old-fashioned elegance. This local tea ceremony contrasted with the worn and undistinguished furnishings, suggesting a cheap let or else a place inherited from parents and allowed to decay because there was not enough money for repairs, not even for upholstery. I couldn't see a single antique or any stylish modern furniture. Meanwhile, Carla took up a position in a corner of the room, at a considerable distance from the two of us seated at the centre. She was mending the green lining of a jacket with absorbed attention, hardly glancing at me and saying nothing after her initial welcome. A long silence followed by further silences almost unnerved me. I felt that Camilla and I were being supervised, chaperoned, as in the old culture.

When Camilla briefly left the room again, Carla addressed me in a whisper:

'Be gentle with our little Camilla because she is such a good child. She needs a mentor, a mature man.'

After tea and small talk there was another long silence. We just sat and listened to the noises of the street through the open window – shouting, claxons, the clatter of something collapsing, a scream, someone singing. This interval gave me time to look at Camilla properly for the first time. I traced the lineaments of her face: refined yet provocative, large dark eyes under swept-back hair, mouth given prominence by the thin, white, almost anorexic cheeks, looking more adult than the impishly hallowed girl I first glimpsed. Maturing, that was the exact word for her, and inviting the unknown, not to be defined. Her eyes returned my scrutiny, mixing melancholy with desire. A thin gold chain and cross emphasised the beauty of her long and slender neck. She was dressed casually – after all she had not been expecting a caller – in a short-sleeved green blouse and short dark skirt, and sandals as before. Bare arms and bare legs, perfectly shaped but somehow visibly repressed, asking the onlooker to be repressed in turn and not to gaze at limbs spotlit by the light slipping through the shutters. That was the rule of our first engagement.

During our next silence I took the liberty to thumb through one of the books piled on a desk.

'Yes, yes, take it, read it!' cried Camilla, coming up to me. 'I read it with my new teacher, but now you must read it too. It is the essence of Italy, beauty, love, everything!' she laughed, and started reading aloud in Italian, with some simultaneous translation and lots of commentary:

'"In a place where there is no light", no light at all, nothing. Isn't it wonderful? They are all there, all the lovers coming together, Semiramis, Dido, Cleopatra and Tristan too, sinning in the flesh, in the second circle which is the proper commencement of hell, now crying all the time, crying because of the pleasure they had once. Most beautiful is the story told of Paolo and Francesca, who only looked at each other for one moment, and then read to each other and saw and loved at once and could never part, because love does not allow any excuse from loving—

Amor, che a nullo amato amar perdona

You see, here is the best part, when they read about Lancelot, and imitate his passion, catch it like a fever, they can't help it, it's irresistible, at once trembling, smiling, kissing. And so, that day they did not read any more. Here, you read it, it's wonderful. Read it now.'

After our silence, she went on:

'Notice Dante does not judge the lovers, and that is good. Of course they are put in hell, because that is the correct morality, the inevitable punishment for adultery. But what you feel is pity. Pity for their sorrow and the cruelty against them, the pity of love. And at the end of the canto the poet who has heard the story of Francesca is weeping. Sorry, do I annoy you? I mean bore you?'

'On the contrary,' I muttered, quite dumb. Camilla laughed with tears in her eyes. Her sister looked up at us somewhat censoriously: 'Don't get so excited! It isn't good for you.' She then declared that they had to visit an invalid aunt, probably true but it came over as a mundane interruption from someone who had no conception of *our* new kinship, a zone of intimacy. Camilla must have sensed this, for as I was being shown out by her sister, she ran up to us and, putting her arms around both her sister and me, said, with a kind of exaltation: 'This is only the beginning, I am sure, it is true!'

★

Within a week I decided to leave. I could see with terrible clarity that it would be torture to stay on, given the extent of my sustained longing for Camilla, every day, every hour, despite the double taboo – her circumstances matched by my new-found reverence for maidenhood. It is true that for some time now I had been fighting my old inclination, not exactly debauchery but a constant undercurrent of temptation. In my new search for pure experience, yes, I wanted something beyond passion and the body. To achieve, at last, disinterested love, not asking for, not wanting anything 'in return' but burning as a martyr once burned at the stake. I can imagine a cynic's comment on that (ageing rake, et cetera) but I owe it to myself to define my conversion. Didn't St Augustine pray, 'Lord give me chastity but not yet'? Well, my prayer was: 'Give me chastity *now* for as long as it takes to win her!' An improvement on Augustine? In any case, in a night of solitary disturbance, the night after Camilla had read to me the story of Paolo and Francesca, I realised that I had to stop or face endless conflict.

Profane desire could no longer be sifted from pure desire. There was a danger of being on fire again; underneath the discipline I could feel the delirium. Insight told me that I might have wanted to do something, I don't know what, but do, do, no longer satisfied with mere contemplation of beauty, with veiled glimpses. Perverse, un-beautiful ideas – perhaps to initiate, test her chastity. I did not have the heart to do that and so I fled in good time.

★

I returned to Florence about two months later under the cover of attending an antique dealers' fair. I just could not admit to myself openly that I had an ulterior motive; I merely thought 'take a chance' – 'perhaps, perhaps' – 'but don't be a fool!' Anyway, when the fair was over, I decided to stay on for a while in my favourite hotel and spend all my spare time roaming and looking. There is an ecstasy of sorts in re-discovering buildings half-familiar from a previous visit, like returning to Santa Croce. I spent hours in front of the tombs – Dante, Galileo, Machiavelli – trying to concentrate on the life and work of those resting there. I tried and tried to chase away the resurgence of my desire. Of course I had a vague memory of the surrounding district; she lived in one little street not far from that great church – but where? A curious local amnesia in the midst of otherwise hauntingly vivid memories. I remembered, or so it seemed, every gesture of hers, the way she turned the page in that book, but I had no inkling of the street name or of its exact location. Needless to say, I had lost the address. (Who arranged that? What exactly did my unconscious want me to do?)

I spent days wandering around the district. Time after time I thought I had found the street but then they all looked so similar, and I could not recognise a single landmark, not a turning, a bar or a restaurant, between the church and the river. I must have walked miles at all times of the day, as if wishing to see how the colour of the buildings is transformed with the shifts of light in the hours between dawn and dusk. I studied the architecture of the balconies, something I have never done before, and visited all the sites of public works, watching the diggers and the laying down of new cables. I likewise scrutinised every face that passed me, including infants in their prams. Once I thought I saw her, her gently swinging gait a hundred yards ahead of me: I ran towards her, I called her name, then ran past her and turned. It was humiliating to see my error. After that I felt that the whole city and all its works of art constituted a vast vacuum. Of course I criticised that feeling, explaining to myself the futile irrationality of my search, but the damage was done. From that time on I felt restless all the time.

One day I reached the church of Santa Maria del Carmine, according to a plan I had made, which dictated a fresh look at the frescoes in the Brancacci Chapel. I knew perfectly well that my wanderings were taking me further and further away from the district where Camilla lived but I forced myself to return to a normal life and abandon a search that might become adolescent and burdensome. I walked into the church, barely glancing at its architecture, restored after a fire in the eighteenth century, and marched with an almost Japanese determination towards my goal in the chapel with the frescoes no traveller should miss. I considered myself something of a pilgrim, or an initiate, at all events distinct from those tourists who came only for ten minutes, pointing cameras at the pictures before they had as much as looked at them. I stopped to focus on the golden folds of the gown of St Peter curing a sick man – head bandaged, hand outstretched – when I saw her, out of a corner of my eye, in a blur, not to be trusted. But the vision turned and spoke:

'So here you are!' She came up to me: 'I was sure you would return to us!'

I mumbled something stupid like 'How so?', confused as if waking from deep sleep.

'I get signs, you know, from above,' she said laughing a little wildly and pointing to the ceiling. 'Infallible,' she added.

'I am studying these,' I muttered, hugging the wall.

'So am I,' she said briskly; 'we all study. *Siamo tutti studenti!*'

I was unable to share her mirth though I tried. Instead, I plotted getting her out of the church, perhaps into a nearby café where we could talk properly. But she seemed completely relaxed in the chapel – in my company but with strangers around – more so than she had been in her home. And she lingered.

'Actually,' she said with a drawl, 'I am drawing this serpent for my group. Look, isn't she beautiful? She! Not it. Look here. Isn't the face of the serpent very much like Eve? Twisting over Eve, watching what she is doing with Adam. Look at the dark eyes and the blond hair of Eve and the serpent. A perfect resemblance, see? Serpentine and suggestive. What do you think?'

I admitted that I hadn't noticed that before.

'But it is so,' Camilla went on, 'perhaps because the

serpent wants to be a beautiful woman. Or does it mean that Eve sees and loves her own image in the serpent?'

'I don't know. Perhaps it is just a mirror image, Masolino's clever idea,' I improvised with some effort.

'Oh no!' she shouted so that heads turned. 'That is a typical, weak, masculine opinion. You want to avoid…seeing how beautiful desire can be evil.' Camilla blushed, her accent growing more marked, carried away by emotion. Who was she really speaking to, I wondered?

'The drama of temptation,' she continued, 'it is wasted on the stupid tourist who rushes in at half past three and sees nothing.'

'I can see it,' I answered, and as I said this I again felt I had entered her emotional world. I thought that was enough conversation for the time being and wanted to leave the church, in her company. But I was treated to another strange rhapsody or doctrine. Only the Virgin Mary could save us from the fall of Eve… 'And when we are tempted, when a perhaps beautiful voice enchants, we must run like an Olympic athlete.'

I wondered whether she was teasing me, as she spoke all this with a smile.

'But you are a guest here and I am annoying you. Sorry. I'm also sorry that we can't invite you now…. Perhaps one day, with my sister, we can prepare a feast for you after all. If you do remain in this city. But now I must run like an athlete, Carla is waiting for me as usual.'

Her smile recalled her first apparition. She hastily gathered up her drawing book and pencils, buttoned up her blouse (a glimpse of her breast) and disappeared. Minutes later I realised that it would be futile to desire, let alone follow her. I just stood there alone in the empty chapel at closing time.

★

I was roused by the impatient stall-keeper demanding to know whether I desired anything. I must have been standing there for a long time, halfway over the Ponte Vecchio, unable to concentrate. I had no aim, no purpose. I suppose that the warm and mellow amber pendant in its round silver setting had held my attention, making me think, simultaneously, of the amber maturing over fifty thousand years in the earth and of Camilla wearing it for five seconds, in a flash of light, her slender neck encircled and emblazoned, the veins in the stone merging with the veins in her skin. But since there seemed to be little or no chance of seeing her again, I spent the best part of entire days doing *nothing*. Certainly there was no incentive to buy anything, or to begin anything new. I was losing interest in my professional pursuits, not looking out for bargain antiques, scarcely bothering to leaf through the catalogues. I was also losing my curiosity about the city and its people. More and more I began to count the hours, the minutes, checking my watch or listening to the church bells strike the hour.

Again I thought I had to leave at the earliest opportunity, but I was being held back, irresistibly, day after day. I considered that I had been abandoned or forsaken, a word that came to mind though I censored it as ridiculously romantic. I kept up the discipline of a two-hour walk along the river, trying to think of nothing, just gazing at the shifting shades of yellowish green in the water. The early bursting into green of the trees, the bounty of Spring in the South, was wasted on me.

I could not empty my mind, still carrying her image as if possessed. Her face would suddenly appear unbidden, as if sketched on the folds of the river. It was always her face, her head alone as if decapitated, I joked to myself. For perhaps I could earn her esteem, and properly prepare for our reunion if I sought only her face, with its traces of unsatisfied desire. To picture the naked feet slipping out of sandals would disturb and complicate my responses. It had been a mistake to glimpse that unbuttoned blouse, even unintentionally. The best strategy would be a Zen-like concentration on some object linked to her but without any appeal whatever, training the mind all the while and learning to see without desire before being permitted to return to her image. When bidden.

Never isolated but always lonely, I kept roaming the streets and the art galleries, occasionally visiting antique dealers in the hope of finding a genuine late Renaissance *cassone*. The only object of interest I saw was a Louis XVI breakfast commode with a rectangular marble top, and a frieze fitted with three drawers and applied with ormolu acanthus scrolls. Needless to say I could not afford it. Most of the time I spent talking to waitresses, shop assistants, usherettes, hotel receptionists, and streetwalkers – chance encounters of a *flâneur*. And still I was unable to decide what to do, I could not force myself to leave.

In such a state of mind I dropped in at the International Club one evening, expecting to be bored by all those hangers-on, rootless foreigners, mostly ageing Anglo-Americans guzzling coke, too lazy to learn Italian or incapable of meeting the natives on their own ground, yet incessantly on the look-out for 'talent' in their vulgar pursuit of a 'date'. I planted myself in an ornate armchair in a corner of the long gallery on the first floor of a modest palazzo, content with surveying the human fauna, observing the assorted wristwatches men and women were wearing, mostly expensive but with tawdry metal straps and hideous oversized digital faces. Quite incongruous in that elegant room with its splendid *seicento* chimney-piece.

Then I saw an arm, delicate, braceleted, dark hair falling over slender bare shoulders. A blue velvet dress. And I could hear her voice. My courage failed, I could not present myself or call out her name. Besides, the recognition was not mutual for Camilla passed me unnoticed, surrounded by a bevy of girls who looked like barely nubile schoolgirls. Among them, Camilla, an apparition once more (I again registered my stupidity but that did not cure my addiction). That moment was enough to renew my longing. An overwhelming concentrated moment – shouldn't that be enough, I wondered? Simply look and vanish, leaving everything else, any step towards potential fulfilment, to chance.

'Donaldo, you here?' I heard a familiar voice, more high-pitched and more Italian than I remembered. The wrong voice. Carla gave me a social kiss of greeting, sat down beside me and immediately started to talk. It took me a while to adjust, to descend from hoped-for music to the simian chatter of a sister. But I remained minimally attentive throughout most of Carla's monologue.

'We come here only to practise English a little, especially important for Camilla, but also for me because I have a few foreign pupils to teach the piano. So here you are. How long? I think it is not good for a foreigner to stay here long. Then comes the disillusion. I have seen it a hundred times, when he get bored even with the Giotto tower because there is not enough patience and not enough love of the place.'

Carla was earnest but she kept smiling ingratiatingly. I noticed her poorish complexion, unusual in an age of cosmetics. But she had sharply outlined features, a good bone structure, as they say, and a fine figure. Perhaps only about ten years older than Camilla, the mature sister nevertheless made me feel that I was being addressed by a matron or a mother superior, a door-woman expecting a fee for allowing me a peep at forbidden youth.

'This is supposed to be a safe place for her,' Carla went on. 'But is it? Who knows? Just look at her dancing! With that bearded young man, Michaele, holding her so tight.

He can't be trusted. And what is really going on in the head of a girl at that age, in this generation? Do you know? Because I don't, I her sister and confidante. She is changing, you know, changing fast. Restless at work. And restless in sleep. Two nights ago I saw her tossing her body and making love to the pillow, well – who knows?'

I was interested but resented Carla's unearned claim on confidentiality.

'I cannot hundred per cent trust nobody in this age. Perhaps you could help, with the language and the reading at least, for you are so old that you are no longer dangerous. People will think you are the father. Or the grandfather?' she laughed. 'And you are a good man, not true?'

I found her tone unnerving.

'The young men so unscrupulous. And she so tender, so vulnerable. But is she naive? Who knows? The literature, the art is good for her. But she is too curious about – other things, everything, you know. Medical books, not her subject, so why? And she is nervous, excitable and melancholy. Irregular. The wise old doctors used to say, marry young! On the other hand I married young and was divorced by twenty-nine from a cruel bastard – he even stole my piano teaching books on which I depended totally. No justice. But I don't want to talk about myself, it is not so interesting, only sad and even bitter.'

I naturally expressed sympathy at this stage but felt still more ill at ease.

'Therefore it is good to meet somebody sympathetic.

Perhaps you could – I mean, you could turn your attention to me?' she added after a pause, smiling. Her voice sounded coy but it might have been just the foreign intonation.

'Anyway I know much more about the beautiful sights than Camilla.'

I said goodbye to Carla as soon as possible and rushed out in the direction of the cloakrooms, hoping to intercept Camilla on her way out. For I had glimpsed her heading that way. However, she did not show up, perhaps there was another exit, just to add to my bewilderment. I left the place disconsolate.

Only the following day did I realise that once again I had received no invitation. And again I failed to track her down. Could I have tried harder? It was difficult as I could not remember Camilla's family name – in fact I never knew it – and I got lost again in the Santa Croce district with nothing to go on except a blur in my memory. I had a vague image of a large, ochre apartment house with obtruding eaves, more of a clue than my previous *niente* but the search still felt hopeless. A private detective would have told me to get lost. Yet I kept circling the area. One day I thought I had re-discovered the elusive yellow house. Eureka! for a moment, then a sense of shame. As in early adolescence, when spying on a schoolgirl from behind a bus stop, a callow Peeping Tom catching a glimpse of red stockings widening above the knees. I saw myself as a peculiarly inane stalker, driven by a base obsession despite my vow of chastity.

Next time I pretended that I had passed her house – was it her house? – by coincidence. It could easily happen, there weren't all that many cross-town streets in the area. Once I was sure that I could see Carla rushing into that house late in the afternoon. For days after that I kept returning, reconnoitring. Then one day, when least expected, when tired out and staring at the pavement like a zombie, I saw her. Dawdling, ambling up to the large varnished front door, lost in contemplation, not looking left or right or in any direction. Head bent, exquisite hands pushing against the door. I felt like running up to her there and then but managed to resist the impulse when I considered how counter-productive my action might be. In any case, I was learning the supposed wisdom of non-action.

On the assumption that I now knew when I could reach Camilla – and talk to her alone at long last – I went back to that house the following day, much earlier in the afternoon, in fear and trembling. Up to the second floor, pressing the bell. No answer. I was about to go when I heard the key turn and saw Carla in the doorway in a sort of shower cap. When she recognised me she immediately took off her cap, smoothed down her hair and greeted me effusively though I must have looked sheepish. I did not feel disposed to meet her, and only her, in place of my fugitive vision. It was a mistake that could be damaging.

I had just enough discipline not to show the extent of my disappointment. Carla offered me herbal tea, which I declined, hoping not to prolong our interview with its prospect of further insinuations concerning Camilla's innocence. So when Carla mumbled something about being worried by Camilla's bad dreams, I hardly listened. Was she trying to imply that Camilla had a bad dream about me? Something frightening, some kind of assault? Later I wished I had concentrated and recorded the exact details. Carla kept smiling even when she sounded menacing. Then she offered to take me around 'the beauties of the land', for the second time. She thought she could find time to drive me out to Fiesole – where I had never been – to admire the incomparable landscape (her words, verbatim), get a magnificent view of Florence halfway up the Via S Francesco, not forgetting the fragments of the Etruscan walls near the Roman Theatre. She promised me a sunny and happy day. Blossoming trees. Spring was here!

I was about to leave when I heard the front door open. Footsteps in the hall, the swish of a bag against our door, and there she was – a surprise entrance, another apparition. I thought she had obeyed my telepathic call. I made an effort to dismiss that thought as folly.

An awkward interval followed when Camilla joined us. I must have lost the knack of a three-cornered conversation for I could hardly manage it. I again felt distracted beyond reason by the way Camilla, sitting on a low chair, demurely pulled down her skirt below her knees. If only she had not made that gesture! Then I would have remained calm, not tempted to interfere, to expose the newly covered flesh. In keeping with my vow, I did not want to be aware of her as an attractive young woman. I struggled to restore her first image. And I struggled to concentrate on what was being said. I bracketed Carla's talk while trying to collect Camilla's spare and scattered words. I could hear the sound of her voice, its tranquil incantation, but not the meaning. I can recall only a few isolated words: 'together' – 'longing' – 'purgatory' – the last one I can be fairly sure of. While talking, she used her hands like an actress, once or twice pointing a finger at me, so that I again felt like a schoolboy suddenly summoned, in the old culture, by a Latin mistress in the middle of a Catullus poem. I remember blushing.

My growing self-consciousness in the presence of Camilla almost cancelled out the joy. So when Carla at last left the room to answer a phone call, I still did not feel at ease, to put it mildly. I even felt an urge to escape, make an excuse, however lame, and postpone my opportunity indefinitely. I managed to resist that idiotic impulse with some effort, but I still could not bring myself to say anything sensible, not one articulate ejaculation. The tension was relieved only when Camilla, gifted with empathy beyond the ordinary, finally spoke to me:

'You are right, words are not necessary. We can listen to the music from the street. And entertain each other in silence. No, what is the word, commune?'

So we sat in silence. At one point she took my hand

lightly, not grasping it, only holding it for a moment lightly, like a virtually weightless object. Her skin had a texture I cannot describe. I had no previous experience of such cool burning, such tough tenderness. Then she placed my hand back on the arm of the chair and withdrew her own body beyond reach. All my previous nervousness lifted and I was drawn into a welcoming space that had no distinct shape. It resembled the traces of a circle, but even that sounds too definite. Time expanded until there was no time. I was astonished when I realised later that only a few minutes had passed.

When recalled into lower reality as Carla interrupted our séance, as I later called it, I was afraid that I would not be able to cope at all. For when I stood up and slowly made my way towards the door, I was swaying as if drunk. But apparently my state was not visible, for nobody remarked on it and I was seen out with due courtesy: the departure of a stranger, perhaps an honoured guest. So I knew that nobody had noticed that I had been shaken to an extent I would not normally call normal.

I lacked the courage to re-visit. I also lacked the determination to leave the city. So I attended to my business more and more perfunctorily, walked around, talked to strangers, and kept writing notes about my shifting fantasies. In the aftermath of our last meeting I desired Camilla less physically, yet ever more intensely – I almost said metaphysically. Nothing else in my world made any impact. I could hardly talk to anybody without getting instantly bored, begrudging the time wasted in polite, forgettable exchanges, even two minutes. I wanted nobody else, no body, no soul.

It was almost dusk on an unusually clouded day, when I ran into her, by chance again. After some preliminaries, past recall, I found myself inside an obscure little church. Camilla seemed to be in a solemn or melancholy mood (a euphemism for symptoms of probable depression). I sat down beside her. In a hushed voice she told me that we were in the church where she had recently come for confession, to a Dominican not old but old enough to understand, very courteous and sympathetic. She paused and muttered something barely comprehensible:

'A little like you, without your secret thoughts of sin.'

She drew back and sat down at some distance from me, saying that it was wrong to break the secrecy of a confession. She remained silent and motionless. Once more I had to try and learn 'to commune' without words, as she had tried to teach me.

After a long while she stood up, went to the entrance of a side chapel, lighted a candle, placed it among many other candles already lit in a row of flickering little flames in front of the cavernous half-light of the chapel. I could just make out the statue of the Virgin Mary clad in a white gown covered with flowers as if for her wedding.

She sat down again, a little nearer to me, again in total

silence. By that time there was nobody else in the church, so I could hear Camilla breathing. When I looked up I could see that her heavy mood had lifted and soon her radiance returned. Her silence gave way to something like a torrent of words:

'It is not a sin to have a nightmare,' she began, 'and I don't accuse you, no, because you were innocent, I suppose. Impudently sneaking into my sleep and touching me. When I was defenceless.'

I told her I was interested in dreams. At that she gave me a reproachful look for the first time, but went on:

'I pushed you into the sea. Then I ran away so fast I didn't see that you were drowning. I fished you out, it was my duty. Your naked body was black and green and twisted. Your rigid hand was waving. I pushed you into the coffin under my bed.'

Camilla started to cry but then said calmly, 'But no harm, in the end, no bad feeling as you can witness.' She smiled benignly as if she had just told me a classic story rather than something intimately personal.

'I suddenly understood that I must wait. Wait longer, wait with patience. Wait without hope. Wait without love, I mean *eros*. And the other love – Father Sandro called it *agape* – is always there, always, without any threat or promise. You know that, don't you?'

Her question took me by surprise and silenced me.

'The moment will come, I have this conviction. But not now, not soon, and not before it is total, mutual, lasting, spiritual, and free from such disturbance. Is it too much to ask?'

I thought she was asking herself and I had no answer.

'My decision is voluntary, not at all a suppression – or what's the word?'

She stood up as if ready to go but lingered, standing before the main exit of the church. I again sensed that she was in no way inviting a verbal response from me, and once more I acquiesced in her wish. I was moved by what she had been saying, recognised its significance, but at the same time I could not be sure whether she was still trying to communicate with me in person. Was she not confusing me with her confessor after all, or addressing a small community of absolute believers, in some holy alliance with her secret vision? I again felt at once attracted and repelled.

'It's not just because of what I promised to my father. He asked me on his deathbed and I promised, it is true, to remain a virgin until I marry.' She paused and blushed, more attractive than ever in presenting her creed of celibacy.

'Yes, I did make this promise voluntarily. I only cried because of father dying, otherwise I felt completely happy. Not yet sixteen, to me it seemed quite natural. But, contrary to what you are probably thinking, I am not superstitious. No, I am a child of my age and I do not accept the taboo as sacred. All right? I am ready to break that promise if and when I am carried away... . But I will *not* be carried away, because the other promise is so much greater. That is what I suddenly understood. The immaculate conception is not interesting for me as a doctrine, that is for the priests, the monks, the nuns… . What excites me is a possible experience – the moment when I am touched for the first time. Touched by the only man on this planet who can do so with so much love and respect that nothing else matters. And nothing hurts or breaks, nothing is stained. No doubt or fear, regret or resistance, no desire for anything else… . I saw this suddenly and clearly as I saw the full moon last night over the Duomo. This is all I can say in a few poor words.'

She turned to me with a look I have not seen before, I hesitate to name that look for fear of sounding naive.

'Go now,' she said, stretching out her hand from a safe distance and grasping my hand firmly, 'go and forget your self but remain my true friend.'

A long time passed, a tedious time, without any contact. It seemed interminable at first when I was still longing to see Camilla but simultaneously I tried to distance myself from her image. Once more I wanted to leave. Our last meeting was unreal. And I could not think of any follow-up that would not be an anticlimax. In the sober hours of waking I told myself that chance had brought into my world a girl who was no girl, perhaps a figure out of memory, perhaps from my lonely adolescence, before I and the age had become experienced or corrupt, borrowed from an alien mythology. At other times I felt only pain and embarrassment about what I had witnessed and I only wanted to annul what she would call 'vision'. But that seemed impossible as long as I stayed on and on in her city, still looking for—

I both wanted and did not want another such apparition.

Finally, I did decide to leave and booked my return flight to London, but forgot to confirm my booking. Then I became ill. Perhaps it was only influenza, but after a week it came back in a second and severe bout, which turned out to be debilitating. Afterwards I felt flat, heavy, lonely, dispirited and impotent.

Gazing at the rippling water of the green river, I realised that I no longer wanted anything: neither to stay nor to leave, neither to see her nor lose her. I informed the hotel reception about the day of my departure and pre-paid my bill in the evening so as to reduce the commotion on the morning of my exit. While I was packing my hand luggage, it occurred to me that the least I could do was to send Camilla a farewell note. Before my recent illness I had started to write a long letter to her, full of feeling, but every word sounded wrong. After two or three hours I was left with a dozen or so useless drafts which I tore up on the spot, defeated and empty.

Then the phone rang and the reception announced a visitor who was waiting for me in the lobby. No name was mentioned.

As soon as I had glimpsed her my heaviness lifted. But I was unable to speak, I merely went up to her, stood facing her at a distance of about two yards, bowed slightly in my habitual manner, and waited. Clearly more purposeful than I, she at once declared that she *had* to ask my advice about something 'terribly personal' and that the reception had just suggested using a small conference room. She added that talking in the lobby was impossible, and that my room was impossible for a different reason.

She began to talk about unimportant things, I can't remember what. But almost from the start, her eyes filled with tears and she was pulling a slightly damaged scarf to pieces, unravelling it thread by thread. Then she spoke with an intensity, in fragments – impossible to recall, to do justice to her quaint eloquence.

'I shouldn't trust you, a man with a past, Carla did warn me, but I have given you…shared my best moments…I hope you remember. Therefore I shall share with you the worst. I deserve punishment, but not so much, not so soon. Do you agree?'

She began to sob and she could not stop for many minutes. I said nothing, and resisted the impulse to touch her hand for any physical gesture of sympathy would have been wrong, that much I could sense. At the same time my desire for her revived, even as I tried to concentrate on her words, eliminating her image, her body, as if she were talking to me on the telephone, on a bad intercontinental line when you still had to wait to be connected by the operator.

'I didn't encourage him, I didn't, you must believe me. I simply didn't run away. Michaele had pursued me, is that the word? As you know I don't even like him, except for the dancing, and I don't really want such poor company, not the closeness in any case. But he knows how to hunt with incredible *persistenza*. You probably did this, I imagine, before you became – as you are now. And there is always a moment, like when music stops the reason, I mean the responsibility. And we are all children, do you agree?'

I think I nodded. While she was speaking, again changing from taciturnity to a kind of verbosity, I said nothing.

'Is it not natural to trust another? Somebody who has not done you harm, who speaks so well, who smiles, is gentle. He even looks shy at a certain point, and in need, and then strokes you a little.'

She stopped and started sobbing again.

'Of course I know nothing about the body, really, very little, because my mother died before I was ten and you know what my sister is like. And books are useless. So I let him, no, I didn't really, I only allowed him to stroke my face and the neck, my confessor once told me that was permissible, if it is affection. But then he touched me, quite suddenly, in a second, less than a second. He touched me there, perhaps gently but violently I now think. I sort of let him, didn't know what to do, in the chaos. That is…'

There was a long silence then she turned and I thought she was leaving.

'Just one question, which is torment: why did I not feel horror then? For a second…it was like joy, I think I cried with joy. Later I realised the horror. But even then mixed, like after a voyage. Of course then I told him to go to hell and I ran home. I think, I hope, there was no physical damage.'

She raised her voice, bent down, rested her head on the small round table between us, and started sobbing once more. Then she said goodbye quite formally – in itself unusual – and left me in a confused state of pondering once more.

★

> I could no longer resist. When she came to me I immediately touched her, the way she had wanted me to. She could no longer resist. The floor split open and our bed fell into the cellar through the huge crack in the floor. I heard a cry of joy amid the sound of crashing masonry.

> I chased Michaele to a filthy garage and cornered him in the half-light. We faced each other and I could see his scornful grin. I kicked him in the crotch with all my strength. Camilla wanted me to do that for her. I watched him crumple up like an empty sack.

> A huge scaffolding covered her house. Nobody could pass. I crossed over to the other side of the street seconds before the scaffold collapsed.

> I could see her lying beside me.

I saw her naked body moving.

I woke from a wet dream, feeling exhausted and despicable.

I woke up again at four o'clock and was unable to get back to sleep. I decided to go out, and walked around the streets like a tramp until daybreak. After six o'clock I ordered coffee in an empty and dingy café but one sip made me feel sick.

★

28th March 1980

Dear Don,

I wanted to write to you a proper letter but impossible. Instead I send copies of something I read a few hours ago. For I value the intellectual friendship between us. Any thought of more would be unnatural, or supernatural, grotesque.

So here I send you:

Catherine of Alexandria was broken on a wheel by the angry emperor, because she refused him, only that, she only protected her chastity. Swords stuck out of the wheel as it turned, but still Catherine was not broken. There was thunder in the heavens and her execution stopped. But after the thunder they murdered her anyway.

(translated from one of my school texts)

I fell in love with Saint Francis of Assisi as soon I came to know him.

The idea of purity took possession of me at the age of sixteen, after a period of several months during which I had been going through the emotional unrest natural to adolescence.
(Simone Weil).

P.S. Don't forget to look at the trees in bud. Why do you always stare at buildings and antiques? You never notice the Spring.
       Baci,
           Camilla.

★

Had I been the victim of delusion? Or folly, the folly of ageing? Of her folly – adolescent, yes, fooling herself and others. Was she making it all up, creating a private soap opera to make life more interesting? Religiosity rather than anything genuinely spiritual? A judge in court couldn't sort out the evidence.

Flying irresistibly into the situation she fears, the proverbial moth into the fire.

Sensuality underneath bouts of juvenile ecstasy.

And in what sense am I her victim? She rekindled the embers of my lust, turning me into a caricature of what I was trying to become. A threat: turning my whole project into something futile. Instead of ascent, a pit. Back into the old rumour or legend.

I jotted these things down at the time. But later I found all that brooding also disgusting. For I wanted only a natural intimacy without any trace of self-consciousness. How else could I have fallen for seeming purity of heart?

★

On the day I finally and irrevocably resolved to leave, I was woken by her call soon after eight o'clock. She sounded excited.

'I'm here already, so come down, hurry! Of course I can't come up. It will be good. No, I can't tell you, a surprise, *importantissimo*. Only today, only now.'

I got dressed quickly, cut out shaving, showering and breakfast. Camilla was waiting for me in the lobby at the bottom of the stairs. Sleepy and bewildered, I let her take my hand and lead me, without a word, out into the street the way she might have led a blind man. We walked like that for an uncertain stretch of time through narrow streets in the morning rush hour. We made our way through the unfriendly crowd. All the while I was getting sleepier rather than more awake and she virtually dragged me until Giotto's tower loomed up with the domed cathedral. A great booming of bells – as if to order – greeted us. Sudden joy.

I more or less sleepwalked into our climb. She called it the ascent, my birthday present (which happened to be another three months away and I don't think she knew the date).

The booming bells enveloped us and we just stood there, neither moving nor talking.

'Wake up!' she shouted into the bell-ringing. 'Up, up!'

The girlish smile of our first meetings returned, then changed into gravity. She took my arm and led me to the entrance of the Duomo, the south-western pier, bought the tickets and led the way in. Flights of winding stairs below me, another flight of spiralling stairs above me, her hair loose and bobbing – that is all I remember.

'I get vertigo. But not when you are here,' she called out.

We continued our climb, she ahead of me. Within minutes I found it difficult to keep up with her but she stopped and waited for me several times.

'Touch the wall. When dizzy.'

I could see her caressing the wall. Now she was out of breath and panting between her phrases:

'think of the builders

'carrying stones, forty floors

'years and years, up

'and up and up

'463 steps, to the top.

'circles all the way

'di giro in giro'

'You need me, as a guide. Not true?' she called out.

She was getting so excited that I was afraid she was going to stumble.

'Circle by circle, *paradiso*.'

Some *'paradiso'*, I grumbled to myself, wondering what excuse to make for getting out of it. If this is paradise, give me purgatory or hell. But I stopped my rebellious thoughts, not wanting to interfere with Camilla's spontaneity, her still breathless speech:

> 'The stairs were dark but
> 'Filippo Brunelleschi
> 'made light for the workers
> 'perpetual fire
> 'flames, salt in oil
> 'and light from heaven.
> 'Santa Maria del Fiore
> 'for her the stairs, for her the dome.'

We had reached a kind of balcony, the base of the Duomo. It was also a resting place. The enormous span of the dome could be seen from there – a void. *The Last Judgement* of Vasari spread across the immense vaulting, skeletons and pitchforking demons jumping into prominence. Was it the fresco that suddenly switched Camilla's mood, a catalyst?

'Dark, light, then dark again,' she panted. 'A dead end, here and everywhere.'

I looked up and saw that she was crying.

'I want to fall – from here. I desire to fall,' she said.

I quietly suggested we should turn round and begin our descent. She screamed at me:

'No, you go. Leave me alone!'

Normally I would have done as I was told but I was getting seriously worried about her new state of mind, as if under the influence of some drug. I told myself that I would willingly quit if only I could find a reliable companion for her, to protect her from vertigo and other fits. Then I hit on the strategy of continuing the climb, going ahead just a few steps and await developments. After a pause she followed. When I turned round I could see her move up the stairs quite rapidly, head held high and body erect. When she spoke she spoke with the old teasing lilt:

'Never look back. And never look at me.'

We continued our climb, hundreds of stairs, in renewed silence. We could see strange little doorways and lesser staircases ascending, criss-crossing lines of construction as in an Escher drawing. Then small, round windows like portholes with glimpses of the city rooftops, a sign that we were approaching the final ascent. Another set of narrowing stairs, then another, until we emerged on the platform at last – astonished.

The normal thing to do would have been to walk around the base of the dome's lantern and take in the magnificent panorama, angle by angle, identifying individual buildings, towers, pinnacles, with delighted recognition: the city and the surrounding hills revealed in sharp detail without benefit of binoculars.

But I noticed Camilla displaying another mood shift. She went straight to the end of the viewing platform and remained standing there, totally absorbed and motionless. Head bent, body sagging, she seemed to stare without seeing anything, for she was staring at the ground or at her own feet – all that splendour out of her ken. She just nodded dispiritedly when I spoke to her.

'It still hurts. The air hurts me,' she said before another long silence.

I tried to direct her attention to the river down there or the tiled sides of the dome immediately below us. The steep rise of the dome made it possible to look down almost directly to the piazza.

'I want to jump over the fence. I want to fall, and fall. A terrible temptation, not true?' she said in a low voice.

In that moment I could understand her wish. Suddenly she came closer, then came up to me, and threw her arms around me with incredible force. She held me motionless for a long time, without a word. When she released me she whispered something I could not understand. Then she made for the exit stairway in a kind of leap, so suddenly that I could not act or think.

I never saw her again.

★

At the airport I got into conversation with a garrulous Italian teacher, a perfect opportunity for a thief. My briefcase had gone, with my journal, postcards, photos and address book. I was left with just a few scribbled notes and those jottings and quotations that I kept in my wallet.

Only the healing pain of memory remained.

II

Married Woman

I think a preface is required here, otherwise I risk being misunderstood, misread even by my friends.

Clearly, I cannot claim to be a defender of marriage, in the sense in which the monarch is irrevocably Defender of the Faith. Nevertheless, I can claim that I have always approached marriage with respect, amounting to reverence for married couples who have stayed the course for seven or more years. My earlier confessions may be searched in vain for traces of pursuing any securely ringed woman, in any part of the world. Chivalry perhaps, courtesy definitely, but adventure – never. Whenever, in the course of my travels, I suspected that I might be tempted by a woman with a guaranteed husband (through her initiative rather than any move on my part), my tendency has always been to take flight, at once. I would likewise keep a distance from any couple about to be joined, in public or in private, and any couple going through a hard time with a sense of potential dissolution in the air. The ambivalence of such states may seem attractive – despite or because of the attendant emotional turmoil – yet I would despise any man who was prepared to fish in such whirling waters. I would judge such a course exploitative and immoral. There remains, therefore, nothing to be done, except finding a relatively narrow strip of fertile land in the terrain otherwise left to lie fallow. It is a zone of sympathy, mutual and intense, guided by the irresistible radiance of another man's wife. To refuse exploring that zone would condemn me to a sense of lasting isolation and impotence.

★

A day of delight I had neither desired nor initiated. To begin with I could not resist one temptation: buying a large box of expensive Belgian chocolates intended as a gift for a friend. Wrapped in silver and gold, peeping out of little wicker baskets or tantalisingly half-open blue boxes with red ribbons, the sheer aesthetic appeal of these bonbons was inescapable. The taste could only be imagined.

Inside the shop I feasted my eyes on variations of the theme, a multiplicity of shapes: lozenges, eggs, globules, delicate cubes, spiralling tubes and (something I have never seen before) triangles building a kind of chocolate pyramid. I got so absorbed in scrutinising all these goodies that I paid no attention to the assistant engaged in tying a ribbon round the small parcel I had just purchased. I was probably vaguely aware of a human shape on the other side of the counter, without being specifically aware of size, shape, complexion, age, manner, accent or sex. However, all that changed when she handed me the parcel, accidentally touching my hand. I felt compelled to look up and focus on luminous dark eyes gazing at me so intently that only some forgotten meeting long ago or the secret expectation of a pending meeting (driven by insidious female curiosity) could have justified such a look. A radiant smile extended to a not particularly prepossessing stranger, a passing customer from the street – it far exceeded the requirements of commerce or good manners. In a rapid glance I could hardly take in her features, those dark eyes turned everything that surrounded them into a blur. I finally managed to focus on her presence and on the spare words she uttered with a slight foreign accent: 'Don't forget your treasure!' she pointed to the counter.

In my embarrassment, I responded with over-emphatic thanks as I picked up my wallet left lying on the counter. I almost lost my composure, I couldn't find the way out, couldn't see the door. It is impossible to recall what I did or did not say in my nascent agitation, probably just ordinary civilities, i.e. banalities. Suddenly I was arrested by her quietly pleading voice: 'We close in less than a quarter of an hour. Do you want to continue? Our promising conversation?'

I must have nodded absent-mindedly, for she came out from behind the counter, hair and hips swinging, gave me a magazine to read and motioned me to an upholstered chair in the corner of the shop. Thus was I transported, in a double sense.

In fact, I tend not to accept improvised invitations, so I made a second attempt to leave. But when I got up to go, I heard that voice again. Could the foreign intonation alone account for its hint of incantation?

'And now you are forgetting your gift!'

Repeated thanks, probably formal, must have followed but I can't remember my phrases, and I can't remember her responses. I can remember nothing. I think I heard an inner command: 'Resist!' That word was spoken clearly and distinctly in my frontal lobes but, in all probability, not heeded further down in the brain.

Out in the street I thought we were about to part when she suddenly invited me, in a seeming-casual way, when I mentioned my professional interest in antiques:

'In that case, I'd love to show you something that's bound to interest you. I do need an appraisal. Can you come, almost at once?'

Her tendency to look me straight in the eye, as if testing the quality of my hesitation, disturbed me. She told me her name, Eveline, and then immediately started talking about herself in a torrent, about difficulties and problems but also prospects. I hardly registered some of her confessional remarks for I was unable to listen properly. Perhaps a few fragments I can restore: 'He is a good man, a very good man, my husband, like a friend or a brother, also my accountant and plumber, my mentor and guide. I shall of course tell him about…this meeting. I detest secrets and men who are secretive.'

We walked on in silence.

'I am no longer looking for perfection. It's the end of youth. Time is my enemy and I can't quite believe in a new life. And you? Why are you staring at the asphalt, by the way, are you addicted or merely feeling guilty?'

I sleepwalked through nameless streets.

I saw the reflections of a violet summer sky on the wet pavement.

I noted symptoms of relapse into teenage state: pounding heartbeat, moderate trembling, thrown back forty years or so.

'*Where* are you taking me?' I asked more vehemently than appropriate.

'To the next traffic lights,' she said laughing.

As we approached her place, I could hear all the old mocking voices trying to counteract the disturbance of feeling again.

★

Once in her apartment, near Wigmore Street, she abruptly but with an engaging smile pointed to an armchair – a fine mahogany *empire fauteuil*. I walked up to and around that chair, placed near the sash window at an unexpected angle, while she went out to the bathroom for a shower. I had time to notice the concave top with ebony stringing above a beautiful pierced trellis-pattern back inlaid with ebony rosettes (circa 1800), when I was waylaid by that voice again: 'I just had to change, I don't thrive in a heat wave.' She had replaced her formal dress with a flimsy blouse and skirt outfit, without stockings. She gave me a warm smile – it seemed genuine. But sobered by the brief interval of my inspection, I at once decided to ignore the ambiguity of such potential messages, and I continued my task, with the single-minded concentration of my discipline: casting a cool eye on precious antiques.

I felt defeated when I could not concentrate, unable to shut out the force of her presence and voice. Was she trying to test or tease me, I wondered?

I subdued my disturbance and resumed the inspection.

The room itself was far from cosy despite its superficial aesthetic appeal. Apart from the chair in question, the furniture was ordinary and surprisingly devoid of soft furnishings. I cannot recall a sofa, any cushions or even a rug. There must have been curtains but when it comes to textiles, what she was wearing alone remains in memory. From the windows one could see only town houses in a long straight street. If there were any pictures, I can't remember them.

She stood behind me silently as if supervising. So I turned round for a moment. As in a film a close-up suddenly creates a shock effect, so now a glimpse of her full figure brought a shocking recognition of her beauty. Taller than I remembered, taller than myself, at least in the platform shoes she was wearing like a tragic actor's buskins.

Whitish face, dilating pupils, light brown hair falling. Dignity with a hint of playfulness, strong-limbed Earth Mother superficially modernised by body care. Dark eyes challenging but tender, without a trace of mistrust. For a fleeting second she evoked the total spontaneity of my virgin friend in Florence long ago. Now under utterly different conditions, I had to send a warning memo to myself: remember that this young woman is married, mature, experienced and anchored, not forlorn, courteous but not a courtesan, occupied by day and night, hoping for a family, a first child perhaps, now expecting the return of a faithful husband whose home this is. In short, retreat before he returns. And abandon all hope before chaos comes. Such simple reflections pleased the periphery of the mind but tended to create turbulence near the centre.

I said I had to go but made no move.

When she offered me red wine, holding out the glass, I could see the down and the veins on her bare arm. I refused the wine, afraid that it might weaken my resoluteness.

'At last I can relax,' she said with a yawn and sat down on the chair that had been the pretext of my invitation, I concluded. 'It's not often that I can do this in company. Anyway, only two can talk. A third person always tends to dilute. Or pollute. But you can get a kind of intimacy when two people talk, like Isabella and Angelo in *Measure for Measure*, do you know it? In my drama department I once played the nun against the seducer, he as hot as an oven, she carrying ice cubes on her breasts. We were being watched intently by a group of actors, nearly all men, getting excited. I mean to say, one of them was getting an erection, it was comically obvious. Just from watching my chaste demeanour.'

She got up, walked to the window and back again, looking at me as if she expected me to make a move.

'The costume designer emphasised my bosom, probably a mistake for this role, I don't know, but I suppose he wanted to suggest the mature woman underneath the lily-white nun. Ingenious in a way, but overdone. Anyway, it had an effect.' Another silent interval followed which she broke by reminding me of my task – the appraisal. 'Back to the wood,' she said, laughing as if she had said something witty.

'Well, yes,' I said, feeling tense, 'I can tell you straight away that the chair you are sitting on is both beautiful and valuable. But I can't put a price on it without further research.'

'That's all right,' she said with a lilt. 'Then you must call later in the week or early next week. Will you?'

'Yes,' I said, troubled by her voice, her intonation again. On the word 'call' the tone of her voice rose. A rite of passage, I thought, without a clear guideline from her.

She again offered me a glass of wine and this time I accepted, thinking it would be rude to refuse once more. After a while she came closer and said something in a low voice – that blur again – something about the peculiar aftertaste of wine, 'I can prove it!' She leaned forward and kissed me on the mouth then, so swiftly that it would be reasonable to doubt the reality of her action. Yet I am sure it did happen as told, for afterwards I heard her say, her voice even lower, the intonation stranger: 'You are shy! It's strange. For surely, you must have had lots of experience, considering....'

A sudden embrace. Her arms gripped me and then let go quite abruptly.

Nobody, no body, had ever felt so light.

'I don't feel really relaxed with you,' she said, 'your arms are too self-conscious.'

This mild rebuke intensified the challenge.

We heard the front door being opened loudly.

'That's Norman,' she shouted, 'at least an hour early.' A classical farce, I muttered to myself, or the tragic discovery of Tristan by the duped king in the darkness. The chance of a lifetime ended.

'Oh, hello!' said the intruder. Queen's English, professional, self-assured touch. Eveline whispered something to him and he greeted me affably:

'Good to see you. A little late but better late than never. And what's your diagnosis?'

We embarked on a prolonged discussion of that chair, and chatted pleasantly enough about antiques with a few travel anecdotes thrown in by him so I wouldn't think that he only wanted to talk shop with me. He was polite, even friendly, smiling without too much effort, not the sort of man I'd normally wish to annihilate. I felt a sneaking respect for his urbanity, which left me guessing whether he suspected anything about us ('us', for the first time) at all. As for Eveline, she touched my hand once, sneakily, while he was looking in another direction.

Both of us were burning, in his presence, as if he had been sent to stoke the fire.

★

In her absence I could see her face more sharply and touch her body more boldly. They used to call the body the house or the temple of the soul, or some such phrase. I shall allocate that phrase to her and in future quote it against all the cynics, and sceptics like myself, to prove the wholeness of bodysoul. What mattered most was that I felt transformed after that meeting and everything else is only story-telling.

I longed for her company — just to be with her for a moment — more than for her touch. But any future meeting had become 'undesirable' in the face of immense complications, actual and potential. Either anticlimax or destructive conflict, within and outside her marriage, was lying ahead of us, at best some diabolic comedy.

★

It was she who took the initiative in ending our separation, after less than a week. I had a tremulous phone-call well into the night, her voice unsteady yet inwardly driven. Again I can hardly remember what passed between us, perhaps only a few half-broken phrases. It is impossible to reconstruct the force of her speech, tentative and winding:

'I didn't want to call…did you want me to?… I had to, in the end…simply to hear what you might… . Don't kill…not yet. I wanted to hear that. I need that. That…yes. I love you too.' After a long silence I heard her say, 'Then why don't you come, just come, at once. I know it's late…the whole house is asleep. The dog? Certainly, and the fish in the tank, and the whole street. The rain has stopped. So come!'

She seemed offended when I quietly pointed out the sheer impossibility of a visit at such a time. She even pleaded and scolded. I clung to my determination to keep fantasy apart from whatever passes for reality, as far as possible. But I didn't want to get into a philosophical argument with her, I wanted to keep things light.

In the morning a much more contained voice answered the phone. After preliminaries, she proposed a plan: a short day-trip to somewhere not too far, I think she mentioned Kew Gardens but the location did not sound much more definite than Xanadu in her enunciation. I was to come to her flat, but not to come in, not come up, not enter the building, use the door phone and wait. She would be waiting, absolutely ready, and come down at once. It was perfectly proper, not a secret, Norman knew about the excursion and had conceded…busy at the surgery until six…best not to tempt fate, no ambiguity, nothing untoward.

Overcoming doubts and imponderables, I got ready very

quickly (giving up my prolonged morning libations) and took a taxi to her street. I walked to the mansions, rang what I thought was the appropriate bell after some search – for the label was smudged – and got no answer. I searched the twenty-odd names displayed along a row of bells and after further hesitation rang another bell, assuming it to be her husband's name, different from hers. No answer. Meanwhile, the obstruction and delay undermined my confidence. I rang again, the third attempt struck a void too. I just stood there not knowing what to do when I heard a male voice through the door phone: 'Who is that?' I gave my name, not prepared to run away like a street urchin.

'Sorry, but there has been a misunderstanding. Eveline has forgotten our wedding anniversary. That's today. So good of you to come. Better luck next time!'

Before that smooth voice dried up, I could hear another voice, in a whisper strong enough to arouse me, 'I need you!'

★

She was in a serious mood when we met in the street. She even managed to look grave, her face set and a little grey, the radiance missing. She informed me at once that she would be very bad company, feeling horrible and looking horrible – unkempt, without make-up and with a small galaxy of red spots on her right cheek. I took this as a new challenge, ignoring the superficial damage and focusing on the underlying strength of her face. In a second her beauty was restored. Her melancholy, or whatever it was, lasted longer. She kept taking our conversation into the darker courts of her being, disclosing her anxieties and fears. She indulged in such an avalanche of negatives that not even the most attentive listener could remember it all. The force of her personality, her voice, mesmerised me. I remember her mentioning, for the first time, her fear of not being able to have children. She said she had always blamed her husband, with an implication of his infertility, or worse. But recently she had a series of bad dreams, about tiny infants, foetuses really, rolling on to her bed wrapped in ice. Then one of her friends, Polly, had a hysterectomy at thirty-five, and that was the end of her, for practical purposes no longer a woman, a woman's life over by forty, and all those ageing women with their face-lifts and hormone replacement therapy were just indulging in ghastly acts of self-deception. It was better in the past when one could go to a nunnery and become an abbess to whom every woman came for counselling. Meanwhile there was nothing for her to do – no job, nothing. Of course she could, yes, she could try, for example get a new agent, but who is to say that she would have any chance. There simply didn't seem to be a suitable role for her anywhere, not even in the provinces, she has moved into the wrong age group, was losing her youth, yes, losing her looks, after all she had appeared on television when twenty-five, that time everybody took notice of her, and it was painful to think how it had turned into a one-off event, worse than…something, something. Her voice tended to fade out, muttering under her breath. At one point she started to cry but stopped herself and looked defiant.

'They just don't want me here, they have decided to block me!'

I countered this with the required antidote, trying to disentangle her chimeras from actualities and, of course, pointing out how absurd it was for her to think of herself as a woman already in decline. I was sure of my ground for by then I had developed a superabundant trust in her presence. As I was speaking, just a few friendly words so as not to suggest a courting speech or a proposal, I must have lightly touched her – touched her hand, perhaps her arm. She immediately turned and embraced me. Her embrace was so spontaneous and intense that I had to reciprocate. Minutes later, or so it seemed, she stopped at the entrance of a shop already closed for the day, and pulled me in from the street into the glass-encircled space there. The kiss that came then was more passionate than any I had ever experienced. Out of breath she said:

'I'm almost at home, but we can't go there. Come, I know a quiet place around here.'

And then she led me, wordlessly and quickly, though the interval of time seemed to stretch towards infinity, to a deserted playground. It was no trouble to enter, the gate was not locked. It was impossible to guess what she wanted – to get on a swing or a see-saw? I sensed a daredevil mood in her and was prepared for some such play. Then she took me by the hand and led me to a wendy-house and almost dragged me into it, into its semi-dark cavity with only a little light filtering in from the nearby street. It was a narrow place where one could only sit or squat on the dusty floor, and we ended up in a tangle, curled around each other, fully dressed. She took my hand and placed it between her breasts and then opened my shirt so swiftly that I was afraid she would rip off my buttons. She spoke not a word and made it clear that she did not want me to say anything either. For a time she was content to prolong our position, then pushed my hand further and further down. She wanted me to stroke her, for a long time, and wanted nothing else, for she even managed to push my body away from hers whilst holding my hand in place. She reached a climax, perhaps not a full one for she muttered, 'Don't stop!' But it was not a place for further experimenting and soon we scrambled out, covered in dust, she complaining of a pain in her shoulder and I banging my head on the roof before I could finally crawl out of our confinement. Soon we said goodnight to each other, rather shyly and unsteadily.

★

She left the town so suddenly that I could not prepare my defences and I was invaded by irrational squads of emotion. I missed her. I missed her so much that I could not respond to any invitation, ignoring at least three 'very friendly' women.

I had already written off the days of her absence as VACUUM and marked the empty space on the map as wilderness. I was unable to re-address myself in any new direction. My desire for her was transformed into pure longing – back to adolescence and to virginal attitudes.

What if I became emotionally dependent on her and lost my sovereignty?

Worse, I had to endure fits of raging jealousy, an emotion I despise and have hardly ever felt before. I began to suspect that Eveline had arranged or accepted a long weekend break with her husband, somewhere abroad – no address, no phone number left – so soon after Norman had officiously interfered with the short trip Eveline and I had been planning together. Was she then swinging back to him? Or was he outwitting me, with scheme after scheme? And was the story of his perpetual busyness, his role as an absentee landlord, a mere cover-up? Was I being deliberately deceived? With less and less attempt at secrecy, *they* were seeing a lot of each other, that much was clear and, in all probability, they were sleeping together again. Or had they never stopped? In that case I have been used as the 'adulterous prop', as 'the fall guy', horrible clichés of our time, just to rejuvenate *their* marriage. And when I had served their purpose, then I would be decommissioned, so to speak.

Worse, I was haunted by the fear that Eveline was becoming less and less available by design. I could have lived with that, practising total celibacy or else moderate promiscuity. But I had a deeper fear that she might no longer be faithful to our vows, and might abandon the high ground of our being together. What if she came to feel that our love was a mere equal of her marriage? Our love would die.

For such love can only live through its own intensity, it has no external support. Passion feeds on itself – it is the psychosis of the sane, who said that? And age intensifies it instead of acting as a moderator, perhaps because the fear of loss is greater. Whilst marriage, I repeated the old adage to myself, is only an institution (she had spoken of her affection for his family – parents, brothers, cousins, anybody at all in the orbit of kinship, including domestic pets) and it thrives on ordinary everyday things, trivialities, doings, even boredom, repetition, the mortgage, the odd visit to the leisure centre and the supermarket and the shared worry of home maintenance.

Against that I had initiated her into a sanctuary, where every moment is significant and every experience new, where we could feel towards each other as in a new creation. And was she now preparing herself to abandon all that, for the sake of those deteriorating routines in an over-established marriage?

What was I supposed to do then? I didn't know what to do so I quoted to myself: 'Wait without hope for hope would be hope for the wrong thing'…I repeated it as a mantra. Yet I could not reach peace. With each repetition of the mantra (and how Eveline hated repetition, or so she had said) I began to long again for her immediate return.

★

Her expected or half-expected telephone call did not come. She was supposed to have returned and yet she did not call, breaking our tacit agreement for the first time, and breaking our telepathy: for her signals and my antennae had, until now, always connected us well before an actual phone call. (Who needs the telephone when we have telepathy? A poor joke but my own.)

And so I had to face my first evening of cowardice for I dared not call her home number. Instead, I improvised some hypotheses.

1) She is back and not calling on purpose, so as to put a distance between us and demonstrate her independence from our telepathy.

2) She is back and longing to get in touch with me but dares not do so, thus sharing my cowardice.

3) Her courage has been dented by domestic scenes, the growing assertiveness, indeed tyranny, of her husband, who has begun to survey her movements. A prisoner at home.

4) There is a power struggle going on while I am waiting here in solitude. *He* has disconnected the phone, ripped the flex out of its sockets, scratched her face and torn the sleeve of her tight dark-blue blouse in the scuffle, then thrown her on the bed and raped her. And she won't have the guts to go to law or even to tell me, her potential protector, about it.

5) She is not back, dared not return for fear of further conflict. She may remain at her undeclared domicile, hiding.

Deprived of her call, I again did not know what to do. I could not play the piano nor attend to urgent business.

In the end I ran around the block five times, hoping that would exhaust me. But by eleven p.m. I was still throbbing with excess energy, driven by the sole desire to see her or hear her. After midnight I rushed out determined to run the three miles to her house, ring the bell and enter at any cost. But I slipped outside my own front door and bruised my left hand and arm to such an extent that I had to turn tail. Afterwards I joked (but only to myself) that *she* would not want to be embraced by a one-armed bandit in the middle of the night when she was asleep, not exactly in 'lap of legends old' but by the side of her usurper. After my fit, in a quiet hour before dawn, I analysed Eveline's absence and her failure to call as unmistakable symptoms of retreat or distancing. It hardly mattered whether she was or was not responding to external pressure. But what if she did stop desiring? Would not that kill all desire, eventually not just my desire for *her* but for anyone or anything? I would be brain dead before the icy hand of the Stone Guest dragged me down – into the void.

★

At last she returned (was it only six weeks?) and we could meet again, two or three times at the old patisserie not far from her apartment. Each meeting was hurried on account of her many other engagements and each time she seemed preoccupied, with money problems and something gynaecological. Then all of a sudden, as she was about to put a slice of cheesecake in her mouth, she blurted out: 'I am sorry I can't feel for you at this stage, that's how it is. You complicate my life and that makes me angry. But I am not hostile.' On the way out, when I moved towards her with affection, she violently repulsed me, there in the doorway, managing quite a street scene.

At this point I should have left her without ceremony and accepted at least one of the unanswered invitations that had come my way. But in the moment of her rejection my longing for her intensified. I considered her still absent and trying to reach me across multiple barriers and obstructions: I glimpsed her faraway smile, I saw delight in her eyes, I drew the map of her breasts under her overcoat, and decoded her negative language to suggest a surreptitious summons. I accepted yet refused to accept her willed unattainability.

★

Out of touch for so long, I lapsed into brooding. How to go on like that, caught between desire and its shadow?

I wanted fidelity above all. But when she pressed me, quite unexpectedly at our next meeting, I simply confessed: a breach. I argued with conviction that sleeping with Jacqueline came not out of passion but out of bad habit. It was an act of substitution or re-insurance.

'I've waited for you so long, in vain. And then body and soul split. Split. Once it was you who made them whole for me, then it was you who separated them. Dichotomised me.'

'What?'

'Split me in two or more pieces. And I can't live like that.

For years I've been fighting those Don Juan urges with some success, and now…'

Eveline interrupted: 'It doesn't matter, forget it. Do you think I care?' she babbled and started to cry in contradiction.

I was afraid that our intimacy had been irreparably harmed. She proceeded to cross-examine me with a sense of urgency: she was eager to know when, where, how, and with whom, in exact detail. I answered as well as I could, minimising the duration (once only), the significance (mechanical or impersonal), the quality (simple penetration, without thrills or frills), and the motive (no genuine desire). Nothing but a hygienic need to prove my virility, I implied, driven by our inadequacies, the excesses of unsatisfied desire she had created: fruitless desire for *her* alone. Perhaps I protested too much. It might be a public service to show, I went on arguing, that the obstacles she herself had improvised had been crippling. In the end, my adventure might prove therapeutic, and if so, she herself would be the ultimate beneficiary, when the time was ripe.

An utterly new feeling asserted itself – guilt. As if I had betrayed her. I saw myself as an adulterer for the first time ever, whilst a harsher voice argued, a little hyperbolically, that I had avenged *her* adulterous marriage.

My confession was followed by contrition. I hoped for forgiveness and absolution. I wanted to offer a new vow of fidelity.

★

An athletic enough start. Two of us running through the streets of the West End in the sudden downpour, laughing at Nature as the prime joker. (Our bodies included under the heading Nature.) It was midday — an innocent hour — when we reached her flat and we almost immediately started to dry each other: she hung my jacket on a clothes-hanger and I started to rub her fine, long black dress with my large handkerchief. Her dress covered her body completely from neck to ankle, until I slowly pulled it back a couple of inches or so, exposing her naked shoulder. Perfectly shaped, and utterly beautiful on its own, it needed no other parts of the body, just as a fragment of Greek sculpture, perhaps Aphrodite's terracotta torso, needs no head or legs to radiate an image of completeness — the fragment of a body dancing. I kissed her bare shoulder, then kissed her skin in the shaven armpit. That simple improvised act transformed both of us, she becoming more quickly excited than I. She moved my forefinger to one nipple, then to her private parts and encouraged it to enter and explore. She exhibited signs of delight in her eyes, in her sounds.

Inarticulate emotions, mixing tenderness with restraint, came in a flood. I knew that we had no time or opportunity to consummate. And I knew that she had encouraged me to do something that she considered 'safe', not just in the ordinary biological sense but morally too. For she would not then have to submit a report, oral or written, to her husband concerning our encounter. Or, if the incident was reported, it would not be taken seriously by his lordship —

governed as he was by sheer materialism coupled with old-fashioned concepts of conjugal rights. He would sharply distinguish between act and play, whilst we knew that in *play* we had joined the Dionysiac dance, the cosmos, nothing less.

I remained fully conscious of the situation as it was – our lying on her great marital bed like figures on a tomb ready for brass rubbing. She seemed oblivious of our circumstances, probably feeling completely innocent.

★

It was nightfall by the time I reached her house, in response to her excited, cryptic call. I obeyed that call instantly though I wished it had come earlier in the day for by now it seemed too late. It was chilly enough for a body to shrink. But the sight of Eveline standing in the doorway renewed my energy and I had begun to anticipate a night of closeness.

She greeted me with a passionate embrace in the hall, an unusual act, for normally it would take her a long time – through talking, changing places and even rooms, a dozen little gestures of approach and retreat – to approximate such intimacy. It took me a little time to realize that she stood apart from me, as a director, willing me to watch and witness a performance. She became highly animated, in excess of her natural vitality, with cheeks flushed, arms waving, voice rising and falling theatrically, eyes shining, posture varied restlessly. She offered me a drink, which I refused, as I always do before a potential night together, but this did not stop her from pouring herself a large glass of something (was it brandy?) followed almost immediately by another glass, and another, gulped down with astonishing speed. Suddenly she began to dance, in her full-length split skirt, a solo act, with swinging pelvis and balletic leaps. She climbed on top of a table and danced on it, beginning to strip like a go-go dancer in a New Orleans bar. She stopped abruptly, jumped off the table and rushed towards me: 'I want you! I have been sleeping alone, doing it to myself.'

Then she tried to lift me off the ground; I did not know that she was so strong and that I was so liftable.

At that point I actually began to move away from her, repelled by the smell of drink and her superabundant sexual display – missing the slow-burning fire and the delicate strategies of our usual delay. But she followed me, put her arms round me and led me in the direction of the bedroom from where, as if acting on a cue, Norman entered. He asked a banal question (something about wearing a dark suit for the party they were going to), treating me as if made of air or gas.

Needless to say, I knew nothing about Norman being in the house or even in town, for Eveline had failed to mention this small matter in her excited invitation. And she seemed to ignore his sudden appearance completely. Instead, she embraced me with ostentatious vigour once more, aware of being watched by her husband, sustaining the position while Norman was in the room and instantly returning to neutral as soon as he had coolly retreated. The whole episode was over in a few seconds, leaving me suspended between disgust and desire.

Love cancelled, for the time being.

The next thing I remember is the roar of traffic and a rough crowd of revellers guffawing in the street. Presumably I had left in a kind of trance, floating out and down that house, hardly conscious of any parting gesture. Did she come towards me with arms stretched out? Fixed stairs behave like escalators when the mind is numb.

★

It was a warm summer evening when we next met – outdoors. Despite all that had happened, I felt re-awakened, mixing memory with stage fright, when Eveline announced on the phone Norman's totally unexpected departure. Something to do with a three-day conference.

At her suggestion we met in the square midway between our homes, still fairly crowded before nightfall – pensioners lounging drowsily on benches, an old woman with enormous swollen, blueish lips, tired-looking young mothers bending over babies, lovers in one another's arms on the grass, midsummer madness tempered by decorum.

Eveline appeared in a long, cream-coloured, lacy dress with a low neckline, exuding energy and freshness. No allusion whatever to her Bacchante act, as I came to call the scene she had created, preferring the classical name to some starker metaphor conjoining the cuckold voyeur and the reluctant stud. Not a word about our weeks of separation, the 'hard time' and the labyrinth of resentments.

Almost immediately we resumed our old ways on one level, talking amiably while trying to explore each other's state of mind. Currents of intense feeling – and underlying tension – began to rise like atmospheric pressure. Even so, she put me at ease, made me feel good in my skin, as the French say, suffused with joy rather than raw desire. I remember thinking that just to be able to feel for her so quickly, after the break, was itself a gift. I thought I saw affection in her eyes, and her body seemed relaxed or preparing for relaxation. But suddenly her eyes narrowed and I sensed conflict again, some yet unspoken anger. Then she looked away, as if to take in the early nightlife of the square – fewer pensioners, more lovers and dogs – and she drew away from me ostentatiously. From her new distance she said something in an atypically grave tone:

'Norman is still here, you know!'

I was afraid that she would somehow produce her husband once more, out of a sleeve or from behind the bushes, and I looked around with mock Sherlock Holmes vigilance.

'I mean he looms between us, can't you see?'

At that I looked around circumspectly, searching the treetops and the space under the bench – where is this spectre? I probably overdid the act, for she told me in a deep-freeze voice that my sense of humour was not amusing, not in the slightest. I was tempted to compare her remark to

Queen Victoria's famous regal snub but became aware that there was nothing fun-loving in her mood. In the darkening light I could see a dangerous, frigid scorn in her looks, as if my very presence had struck her as a hideous provocation. I think I tried to say something conciliatory to avert another failure, another sad taboo on tenderness.

But she was once more out of reach. She just stood over me stiffly, and addressed me with cold formality and barely concealed rage:

'Perhaps he left on this journey to escape. Because he knows. You think you are so diplomatic or noble or whatever, but you are not innocent. And *he* is suffering – a much better man than you – working for me and others, that's altruism, not your egotism – that's why I'm so free – that's how I was able to meet you and befriend you – that's all I wanted, nothing else, perhaps a hug and some good talking, I didn't want the rest, yes I did, but in myself I did not want what I wanted when with you. And you sit here looking so old, limp and bony – so how dare you come between us here and interfere…'

'You invited me. You took the initiative,' I muttered, something like that, but memory begins to fail.

She continued her speech, angrily contrasting her husband's virtues with my failings. I said next to nothing but stumbled on a word that must have sounded to her offensively ironic – was it 'a paragon'? – for her rage became open and violent, and she started shouting at me, incomprehensibly, in that public place. The pity of it, the terrible pity of it, on the night of our one and only chance to be together, I thought. Yet I slapped her face then. She lifted her umbrella and thrust the pointed end into me with force (under the navel, no damage to the genitals, I diagnosed). She immediately started running while shouting for help to a couple lying on the grass: 'He's attacked me, help me!' She ran at speed through the iron gates of the now almost deserted square.

Slowly I went home, what else could I do? About an hour later, towards midnight when I was almost asleep, the phone rang. Her distant-sounding voice whispered something barely audible, like 'Nothing to say, night.' Then she said, more clearly but in a very low voice, 'Sorry about this evening but not sorry. No apology, no, only it is such a pity, generally speaking.' Pauses, silences, fragments of speech: 'I miss you already, but then I don't, not at all. I had such a good shower and…I've gone to bed. I really wanted to sleep alone. I wanted…company, but now I don't, I've stopped caring altogether… . I can't, I can't!' Her voice faded out. I said nothing, perhaps just echoed some of her isolated monosyllables – 'want', 'miss' – in a broken dialogue that makes little sense when the sound of her voice and her quickening breath are not heard.

'Then come now, come!' she whispered abruptly and put down the receiver immediately.

I was on the point of calling back to ask her for confirmation, not wishing to be a victim of caprice or hallucination in the middle of the night. I sat down for long minutes to confront this dilemma but no thoughts came. In the end I got dressed, ordered a taxi, which was slow in coming and strayed miles beyond the street I named. It was past one o'clock in the morning when I arrived and rang the bell. There was no reply.

After a long wait she let me in. I found her dressed as if for a party in a dark-blue, full-length gown and outdoor shoes, with make-up. As soon as we were in the sitting room, she sat down in the famous chair of our first meeting and pointed me to a plain Windsor chair at the other side of the room. There was a long and awkward silence. Then she informed me that she had made a mistake, she had invited me in a moment of mental aberration, feeling perverse, but as soon as she had caught sight of my scarecrow face emerging from the dark hall she realised what a fool she had been. She hoped that I didn't expect anything from her. She advised me to leave at once to avoid further unpleasantness. She didn't enjoy saying such things but it was better to be a hundred per cent honest – just to be under the same roof with me disgusted her. She did not want anybody else either, she added by way of a palliative. Everybody was disgusting. That's horrible too, and somehow I had brought out the worst in her, something diabolic nobody else did…

I heard an echo of some earlier phrasing of hers, 'You bring out the best in me, nobody else makes me feel like that.'

After another long and awkward silence she got up, turned off the spotlight and left the room without as much as a goodnight. Deflated, I sat there in the gloom for an interminable stretch of time, trying to gather enough energy to leave those premises with some scrap of dignity. But then I obeyed a contrary impulse and very quietly, almost furtively, opened the door of her bedroom, determined at least to part in amity. She was lying on top of the double bed, still fully dressed but with shoes off, eyes closed and motionless. I sensed that she was not yet asleep. But I could not hear the sound of her breathing as I approached and she did not move, made no response at all, when I touched her lightly. I stood over her for a long while and then lightly touched her again, her bare shoulder, the only exposed part of her body and said goodnight *pianissimo*.

'Wait!' she said as I was leaving, and I turned back, watching her prop herself up on a pillow with half-shut eyes.

'This is ridiculous,' she said in a low voice. 'I feel nothing for you, nothing at all. Yet last year I had a fantasy – a scene just like this, you came to me like a thief in the night and you just lay down here, yes, and we went to sleep together. We slept in perfect peace and then towards morning I encouraged you and you began to stroke me, inside my thighs and on and on, my clit, and we stayed together all morning.'

I could see that she was getting excited and when I touched her in the armpit she pulled me down to her. But she immediately pushed me away again, with such force that

I landed on the floor. I lay there in pain for a few minutes. Torment of love unsatisfied was followed by an odd feeling of exaltation, a self-congratulatory salute to Gawain, the chaste and chivalrous knight who had defeated what was left of the Don.

Eveline must have enjoyed this scene in a way for she said, as if by way of compensation:

'It was good you came after all. But go now. Don't expect any encouragement from me. I hate the male orgasm in an ageing man. Why can't you be just my guide and confidant?'

★

It must be admitted that I got really disturbed when, about two weeks later, the front door bell rang before seven o'clock in the morning. I was not fully awake. My nightmare lingered, the impact of long, labyrinthine corridors, with friends standing by like sentinels calling out 'Fool!' and something like 'What what, what, what did you expect?' When the bell rang again, and then for a third time like an alarm, my first impulse was to ignore it and wait until the disturbance ceased. But finally I gave in, opened the front door, and found myself confronted by Eveline in an overcoat, carrying a suitcase and a travel bag, and smiling in a way we tend to smile at the porter of a government department. Nothing personal, no greeting.

'Why are you blocking the doorway?' she asked sharply. 'Can't you let me in?'

I obeyed and waved her in. She dropped her luggage in

the hall, moved into my sitting room and sat down in an armchair without a word. Long minutes passed without a word, in a haze. There was something in her face and posture that forbade anything approaching an interrogative opening from me. After a long silence, Eveline said, just audibly:

'Let me stay!' After another silence she added, 'A short time – a few days.'

There was a garbled reference to some domestic fight, so indistinct that I might have merely imagined it in my effort to find a motive. After a while she let herself down to the floor, and sat there, still formally dressed, as if waiting for an audition like a young actress who wanted to be noticed yet seem 'natural' at the same time. Tense yet controlled, rehearsed yet possibly spontaneous.

'It got quite simply claustrophobic, unbearable,' she said under her breath. 'So don't keep looking at me like an inquisitor. Get dressed and do some work!'

I didn't know how to respond to this, repressing phrases like 'sorry to hear that' and 'you'll make it up in a day'. I must have given her bromide or worse, for suddenly she flared up and shouted at me:

'That's it. I might have expected it. You unchivalrous shit!'

I patiently explained that, while she was welcome, the complexities of the situation had to be borne in mind. It was in *her* interest not to do anything foolhardy and irrevocable. That would end her freedom – our freedom –

to follow up potentialities, and all the delights of interplay, as the spirit moves us. While speaking, I glided towards her, wanting to comfort her with some gesture, perhaps touching her, in a light embrace. I also wished to postpone further talk until she had calmed down sufficiently to be open to wise counsel.

But she did not want to hear me out, had no patience. On the contrary, she shouted at me again with uninhibited fury.

Then she picked up a heavy glass paperweight (more decorative than useful) and held it over my head. I froze on the spot, unafraid. After a long minute she withdrew her hand and replaced the glass object, muttering, 'You nearly had it this time!'

Though not normally concerned about my neighbours, I half-expected some residents from the other apartments to burst in and make inquiries, offering help, calling the ambulance or the police. For it must have sounded like a terrible row, even though it was essentially one-sided. Nobody came.

I was trying to find a way of throwing her out without damage when I suddenly developed an unusual degree of guilt, as if I had actually been responsible for her distress. I wanted to repent, reverse my attitude and let her stay on as long as she wanted – throwing caution to the winds. But she came up to me with an ugly expression in her face, impersonating a wounded creature; she made a hissing sound, then turned away from me, clumsily collected her luggage and rushed out through the front door. I could hear stamping footfalls descending the stairs.

★

Despite everything, I was thrown back into the whirling pool of limitless thinking about her and the ripples from that pool were enough to satisfy me, for the time being. Desire for further adventure was totally suspended; I sorted the memories I had stored up.

I have to stress this only because hardly anybody will believe me, and with the passage of time I can hardly believe it myself. I am not claiming that I had, in the meantime, utterly forgotten the shape of her body – the time when I folded her thighs back into a frame for her lifted face. But my strongest memory is of a person discovered at each new meeting as if for the first time. Then her wild unpredictability could be seen as just a series of spontaneous impulses. How to prevent them from turning destructive?

Once the illicit idea occurred to me that we might have been joined in some ritual, in sacred nuptials, perhaps in prehistoric or pagan times. Historically speaking, we had known each other for about two years by then, surpassing all original predictions.

More than once I was afraid that our imagination could die.

★

After a long pause I decided to phone Eveline, hoping that

I would find her in a good mood, perhaps tender and responsive. I wanted to hear certain undertones in her voice, and certain wordless sounds between insignificant words. I called at the time she had suggested, neither too early nor too late so as not to risk further disturbance or hearing the voice of someone else again. So I phoned early evening. My call was answered by Norman.

I almost lost my composure for his homecoming was not scheduled for that hour. But we managed to exchange a few ill-chosen words of icy politeness, mostly concerning this or that antique bureau, for the tenth time. Finally I plucked up courage to ask if I could have a few words with Eveline (on some credible but mumbled pretext) to make it all seem natural, despite the reality. Also I hoped that just one word or two from her would cure my restlessness and heal the malaise. For a minute or less Eveline seemed to listen to what I was muttering. Then she interrupted me abruptly and poured into my ear an unexpected message: 'It's too late, and you are disturbing us. I hate your call. And I hate you!' she said hoarsely and slammed down the receiver.

The pain got worse through the night. A psychic bruise behaves like the physical sort, it can be ignored or belittled in the moment of a fall but then it grows. It grows over the week, into a lurid multi-coloured phenomenon, throbbing like a drill. I tried various short-term cures at that stage, such as cursing her for the first time to exorcise the demons, hers and mine. But exorcism is far from easy, and to do it unaided is like trying to lift oneself off the floor, levitating towards the stratosphere.

★

It was about that time that I first started composing little messages not sent:

To her: 'I accept your infidelity, but not your indifference. Were you drugged?'

To him: 'False Pretender! Petty Karenin!'

These scribbles, with many others, failed to relieve me, and after midnight I had to choose between a sedative and whoring.

I chose the sedative.

★

It was about that time that I wrote one more letter to her, the one I didn't send:

Eveline,

What I said to you does not imply a lack of respect for your new-found fidelity in marriage as such. I really hope that you will thrive conjugally, seeing that you are putting so much will and effort into all that maintenance work.

And yet I find – this is going to be difficult – certain expressions you have lately started using ('I love Norman'…'I must not hurt him') excessive. Alas, they sound conventionally Victorian both in attitude and wording. Where is the adventurous, open-minded, imaginative, recklessly passionate young woman I came to know?

No, the abyss between marriage and *eros* cannot be asphalted over by a simple repair job, as you now seem to believe. Marriage, even as its best (and *is* yours among those?) dwindles into a convenient arrangement, a bastion against the intrusive external world and, yes, the routine performance of the sexual act seldom remembered the day after. Within eight years (note my generous addition of a year to the proverbial seven, for your sake) repetition and habit tends to kill intensity.

Set against that our boundless desire.

The torment of being for ever unsatisfied, and the agony of our emotional conflicts, have kept us going in a true adventure, when every moment is timeless and every motion perpetual.

So I accept your stern taboo, I accept it and all the other repressions that follow. I have the curious feeling that I can remember an endless future with you.

Don

P.S. Cancel all I had written. Nothing and nobody, neither crisis or conflict, nor bouts of anger and misery, can separate us from each other. Only our own inadequacy can come between us. But then our inadequacy seems paramount.

★

A new dimension. Inexplicable then, and it still is.

Perhaps I had failed, missed a certain expression in her face, a nuance, in that restaurant's pervasive cloud of cigarette smoke. Perhaps I merely missed a word or a sound, something she had said in a low voice in the midst of the surrounding cacophony, some attempt to tell or warn, a half-hint. Whatever the omission on my part, there still remains a disturbing puzzle about the abruptness of her treachery, even by her own standards of unpredictability.

As far as I can remember, and the main impressions are firmly etched in memory, we sat at table eating a good meal in a tolerably relaxed state. I was trying to anaesthetise the previous pain; she sat in silence, looking her best in a deep-cut black dress, in no way immodest, a white velvet band around her graceful neck with an amber-and-silver pendant under it. She must have attended a function late afternoon or was heading for another function late in the evening (we arrived at about eight o'clock). The details matter less than my overwhelming awareness that, despite everything, she had not lost her power.

Our talk was mostly light, avoiding personal topics as far as possible. I remember feeling grateful that we were at least together again, in some kind of equilibrium. After gulping down several glasses of claret, Eveline made a derogatory remark about her husband, which surprised me, after her recent worshipful attitude towards him. She then muttered something about how she wanted to phone a fascinating new friend, but she remained seated and we went on talking for some time in an animated way. The noise level of the music was constantly rising. I felt a tension without immediate cause in the longish silence before I could distinctly hear her say: 'I want to make love!'

I have never heard her say that before, the explicit phrasing if not the thought was quite new, not her style. So I sat up and took notice. I could see that her face was flushed and her eyes over-intense. I went out to the cloakroom then, taking the opportunity to increase my daily dose of Vitamin E. When I returned to our table, Eveline was gone.

★

I was woken in the middle of the night, not later than four a.m. I struggled to get up, stumbling across a dark space, tripping over the flex of the telephone. I could hear nothing at all when I lifted the receiver and I remember feeling so angry that I wanted to smash the instrument itself. At least the anger cleared the buzz in my head. Finally I heard the sound of rapid breathing. Somebody's practical joke? I could also hear an indistinct male voice in the background and music, a heavy beat subdued by distance. This went on for long minutes but I could not bring myself to end the session of torture. For I thought I had recognised the quality of her breathing, and something in me responded – a mixture of chivalry and masochistic curiosity. Time passed, I heard a click, and I was on the point of giving up when the voice spoke:

'I want to tell you…it is very, very difficult…but I am not ashamed.'

There was a long silence, a lot of breathing and sighing and a kind of blowing noise as after physical exercise, jogging or swimming.

'It's crazy, I know, but I couldn't help it…not any longer… . I held back for days, weeks, I refused to see him… . No, not Norman, of course not, he doesn't count. I am with (an incomprehensible name)… . I did, I did, I certainly hinted, I tried to…but you are too traditional and stupid…and I need to experiment while I am young…more than you. Of course he is younger than you, or me…like you in some ways, travelling and bizarre…but he has the skin of a boy, lovely. Please don't start moralising…I need understanding, support… . No, I am not hostile. I am kind of grateful…you showed me the inadequacy of my marriage… (She started to gabble, which was unusual.) Now I can play the Don…don't you feel flattered? (She was laughing into the phone speechlessly, making a hideous noise.) Anyway, it's exciting, but serious.

'You are so stupid!' (She slammed down the phone.)

★

The next evening I made a phone call, which was answered by Norman in his usual courteous and detached way. We kept up a conversation, maximally impersonal at first. But I remember suggesting – partly to fill in the time while I was waiting for Eveline to take over the call – that we should perhaps have a good talk over drinks discussing matters of mutual concern. I felt empathy for him that time, seeing an opportunity for us to become friends. I hinted (but did he understand?) that in any marital crisis he could count on my support and help, if such a thing was possible. It might be impossible to influence a frantically strong-willed person in the direction of stability and common sense, rather like taming a tiger. We chuckled, but not very heartily.

Meanwhile, Eveline did not come to the phone. I so much wanted just a few words with her – to enlighten and reconcile. I had to couch this desire in an indirection: 'I suppose Eveline has gone to bed by now?'

'Oh yes, she has,' Norman replied, 'but not in my bed.' I expressed some dismay and ended the conversation.

I had one final and minimal telephone conversation with Eveline the following morning. She was impatient yet eloquent – said something about 'the chance of a life-time' and quoted 'the road of excess leads to the palace of wisdom'. She said she was prepared for divorce if... . When I raised an objection, she shut me up. She said, 'Couldn't you just evaporate?' and finished without another word.

★

It was a unique experience for me: an absolute refusal of the mind, and of the body, to accept her disappearance. In face of such an event three decades of my worldly wise practice proved inadequate. Her absence announced itself as an emergency, disturbing almost beyond control. End of the comedy, only loss felt. After the first hour of acute pain, I was chronically drifting from place to place in an increasingly hopeless search for traces of her, looking for footprints. Day after day I was driven like a leaf or a cloud, the will suspended (aware of those pale romantic images as grotesque). Driven from place to place by the desire to end desire. At least that is what I told myself: I would be cured by one final glimpse, a touch and then a decent ritual of departure. A little ceremony of farewell. Then I would be ready to abdicate with dignity. I would have reached something like an alternative consummation, compensating for the failures of our self-cancelling love. Have I been punished because I had delayed, had held back – at her command, her preference for endless deferment?

I needed to know more, and so I set out on a kind of quest.

I strayed into that part of the town barely conscious. I looked up and saw before me the playground which I had not seen since that time, when she led me into it.

Addicted to walking long distances without any clear sense of direction, I was no longer searching for her with any sense of a goal. It had become purposeless drifting. There must have been some reward in arriving at this or another site to watch the re-screening of an otherwise vanished episode, in grainy black and white with shadowy figures almost stumbling across the scene. Then a moment of half-recognition, together with the relevant pain.

It was a narrow place. Inside a large wooden box, with hardly any elbowroom, I had to crouch so as not to be hit by the ceiling. The size of a large dog-house, not intended to accommodate adult humans. I felt totally out of place there. Despite considerable physical discomfort – aching shoulders and knees and a buzz in my ears – an unexpected sense of well-being visited me as she held me once more in that narrow place with naked arms. Out of breath and radiant. It lasted a moment.

Suddenly a group of children started yelling at me, pulling and shoving me even after I had managed to climb out of that confined place unaided. I stood stock-still in the midst of those screaming children. A pompous old woman with an ill-fitting woolly hat (I was still fixated on the summer, hardly noticed the cold) upbraided me. However, I did not feel humiliated. On the contrary, I scrutinized the hag's Rembrandtesque wrinkles for signs of benevolence and I tried to pacify her with a soft answer, an explanation of sorts. I then asked her a few pertinent questions, finally putting to her the inescapable one: 'Have you seen anyone (brief description) visiting this playground lately?' It soon became clear that the old woman had absolutely no recollection of anyone or anything significant, possibly a case of senile dementia. It was also perfectly clear to me that it would have been futile to look for traces of footprints in the dust of the playground.

I can affirm that I remained sober and restrained in my exit, *unlike* the famous wanderer who went on looking in vain for traces of her footsteps in the snow.

★

I saw her, I am sure, not very far from the hotel, scrambling up those sandstone cliffs. I saw the back of her head first, unmistakable after the terror of half-recognition, her delicate neck exposed, head tossed, hair falling, hips swinging, studied insouciance, faraway closeness. Nobody could impersonate or copy all that.

I did not know what to do: call out, follow her up the steep ground, remain standing where I was only a few feet up the cliff, or (wisest of choices) retreat before she could turn and perhaps glimpse me from the heights. After a wait, when I had almost lost my concentration and my focus, the climbing figure stopped in her tracks and looked around to survey, it seemed, the whole panorama, the bay, the headland and the ebbing tide. She seemed to spot someone invisible to me and waved. Then she changed course in that direction and began her descent with surprising speed.

A kind of paralysis held me, sometimes seen in animals, in a cat trying to cross a major road at night, trapped by the headlights of an oncoming car – crouching as if unable to move either forward or backward. I could still see her figure descending towards the unseen person. Finally she waved again, waved her whole arm vigorously, and, almost skipping, ran downhill towards him.

She had reached him and together they ran down the rest of the cliffside or into the rough grass, in a blurred perspective.

Again I did not know what to do. But since there is a time-limit for purposeless waiting if one is to retain a semblance of sanity, I quit. I consider it genetically given that a man should strive to bring a search to some kind of an ending.

III

DIVORCEE

The lift stopped on the fifth floor, and she got in, simultaneously speeding and stalling, her initial effort at entering fast awkwardly checked by getting her bag entangled in the door of the lift. Even so she seemed unruffled and she found the time and energy to accost me – that's how it seemed – before we reached the fifteenth floor. 'Snap!' she said, holding up an exhibition catalogue identical with the one I was holding. 'Snap!' she repeated. 'This is fun.' She claimed to have recognised me from an antique dealers' fair in Fifty-fourth Street and announced that we were sure to meet again – sure? – at the final dinner. She gave me her visiting card with a lot of information (including her e-mail address, at that time not yet common), a brochure advertising an exhibition she was organising, and an invitation to the opening of a small downtown showroom.

    I don't think the minimal encounter would have registered

in my mind – so many meetings compressed into a few days in that turbulent city – if she hadn't behaved so oddly in the moment of our parting.

'It was meant to be,' she said emphatically, 'I know it. Once in seven years.' Then perhaps because she had observed my inability to respond, she switched to the usual-casual register: 'Excuse me, I'm a bit uptight today. Take care!'

★

It was inevitable that we should meet again. In other words, only by making a special effort could I have avoided her. And what could have been more self-conscious than that? Back to the bad old days of youth: distancing when approaching, indefinitely postponing what's desired, creating fresh obstacles, et cetera. In the end I went to that banquet without any expectations. About a hundred people were present, I knew at least a dozen of them quite well. So there was no reason to privilege a newcomer, and it wasn't I who had arranged the seating plan – she next to me at our round table for eight. It was chance, the banal but not neutral lottery.

Clearly, I am not beginning this story well, for telling it like this puts me under suspicion. They will say: he would not protest his indifference at such length if he had been truly indifferent. Yet that is how it was. If there is such a thing as 'telling the truth' still, then I must try and practise it, even if I have to dig deeper and risk disbelief. I could hardly talk to *her* at the banquet at first, there was so much conviviality: the conversation rising beyond shop and gossip, into flights of debating and story-telling, accelerated and perhaps deepened by wine, brandy and coffee. Suddenly everybody was likeable, lifted into a state of amity, euphoric enough to be disposed to accept the universe, for an hour or so. I still remember the repeated bursts of loud laughter though the jokes were inaudible. I also remember Louise, an old acquaintance sitting to my right, complaining cattily that she couldn't get a word in edgeways because 'you seem to have got lost in that woman's dark-dyed hair'. It was the kind of remark that one would normally dismiss as trivial teasing, but it was given a memorable edge when Louise added with bitchy nonchalance, 'How do you manage to pick up such beautiful old women anyway?' I retaliated with something even more unpleasant – 'at an antique dealers' market', or something like that. Sudden laughter accompanied my feeling of guilt. At least I felt relieved that this exchange could not have been overheard by *her* in the general din of the banqueting hall.

In a sudden change of mood I thought, to hell with all this superficial socialising, and turned to my new companion, hoping for something more genuine. There was a kind of stillness about her, a smile not pre-arranged for an interview but seemingly beamed in my direction. And she did not look old, on the contrary: a girlish profile, high cheek bones, ripe lips, and her dark hair (singled out for jealous comment) curled round her small ears in ringlets. The hair was dyed in all probability but it was impossible to guess the original colour. When she finally stood up, a slim and lithe figure revealed itself – she might have been in her early fifties. Anyway, she had poise, and I felt drawn to her sufficiently to act on a strong 'let's get out of here!' impulse. So I found myself outside the main entrance, with her, before I had time to think, analyse or plan. A taxi drew up. Did she flag it down? She must have done, for I made no move, of that I am still convinced. We shared the taxi for a short time, driving north, then stopping somewhere beyond 50th Street, outside an old four- or five-storey brownstone. She said something very quietly, tenderly, breathless words I could not hear though I heard their music. Then she leaned over and kissed me on the mouth, her tongue in my mouth for a fraction of a second. She sighed and, almost immediately, before I was fully aware, quickly opened the door of the cab and was gone. She didn't wave, she didn't look back, just disappeared in the poorish light of the street.

I ordered the taxi to drive on to my hotel and pretended that nothing had happened. I mean, I classified it as a passing episode, and her as a generous American woman probably making a habit of that sort of thing.

★

The following morning I was woken by a phone call, too early by my standards, before eight a.m., I think. All I heard at first was a voice, a voice without words, again, a quiet voice with some vibrancy, a light quavering. (I am very susceptible to the nuances in a female voice, I have discovered as if for the first time, though it has happened before, no doubt.) Eventually, her phrases crystallised along the lines of: 'Sorry to wake you, Don…I could be your guide…your first time in New York…I have a kind of plan for you.' Then a blur, then a list of her errands – something to do with a friend getting a divorce, another split, separation or division, 'inevitable, the curse of our time, an epidemic and there is no known cure for it', I think she said. Hard to recall the exact words. I was concentrating on her instructions, where to meet (at a cafe I would easily find) at noon. A safe time for someone who wanted to avoid an adventure. Avoid the hours after nightfall, when the owls of Minerva take flight, along with other flights. Apart from anything else, I had to leave in less than a week. More importantly, I had my own agenda from which I had no desire to be distracted. Besides, my one-time courage had been thoroughly undermined by Eveline's betrayal. Who wanted another round of ridiculous torment? There was no point in lamenting the past, the waste of it. But it was high time to switch to commonsense, to cautious detachment, and so I set out in a no-nonsense mood to meet Amanda – the first time I called her by her name.

I let her lead me. You might as well say I abandoned myself to my guide, and why not? My caution did not have to cover the ordinary affairs of the day.

The lift was so quick, it did not leave enough time for full consciousness. A precipitate ascent. We reached the top in seconds, with troops of children thrilled by their fear, holding on fast, fingers in their ears against the rushing sound, the compression of the air. Suddenly we were up in a shock of surprise on floor 107, on one of the twin towers. Not much turbulence but it was too windy to go out to the outer perimeter. Viewing the vast city jungle of towers through glass left one feeling secure for a moment. No, not secure, for being higher than Babel, higher than anywhere at any time, engendered a fearful feeling of transgression. Danger mixed with a sudden sense of achievement when we reached the top, almost as excited as the children in a first adventure. Amanda went pale and leaned against the glass.

'Don't you feel, don't you think…?' she began and seemed to fade out. 'Simply to end,' she said. 'Fall, all the way down. Down, and finish the whole story,' she said. I looked at her, her white face, sinewy and drawn. Then she burst into tears and blubbered, 'Never mind, it's foolishness. It's been such a week, so much is going on, as you know, you know, don't you?'

Did we jump and fall all the way? Then wake, slowly regaining consciousness. When we set out for a long walk northwards, neither of us seemed steady. She stumbled, said something incomprehensible, and cried. Within minutes we regained a degree of rationality. I remember that she started telling me a story about somebody who had to be physically restrained by a friend when about to jump from the bridge, rescued against her will…

We nearly got run over by a reckless limousine, or we were reckless by not heeding the traffic lights. Our long walk in the autumn light resembled the descent from the tower, it was effortless like a fall. I can hardly remember walking through the Village, and that famous, neglected but potentially beautiful square, for I was concentrating on Amanda all the time. I sensed that she was on the brink of crying again. We circled around Gramercy Park, glimpsing the statue of Edwin Booth as Hamlet, in a slow promenade.

'There, in that direction,' she pointed (towards Park Avenue South?).

'In the middle of the night…without warning…perhaps he had met someone else…or he just flipped. Raging like a gorilla…he pushed me into the rain, into the street, in my nightie. I had no time to dress, to take anything, anything at all, just an old handbag, no money or credit card. Nowhere to go, not a friend for miles…out of my mind, battered. Without a cause, you know, he wouldn't talk, wouldn't explain. Less than two years together, my third marriage, it had begun so well, in harmony…he had real talent, was attentive, seemed mature. Surely there is no need to make love…every day, at that stage, the famous midlife …and…nobody can live through that sane, you couldn't, Donald, and I couldn't, of course not.

'Will you stop smirking? Or are *you* a sadist too?'

'Sorry, sorry,' I stuttered, 'I wasn't aware of any expression. I feel nothing but sympathy.'

'I don't want your sympathy!' she shouted. 'And now you sound just as unctuous as he did, before violating me.' She stopped crying. 'No, I'm sorry. I shouldn't…. But every corner throws something at me. Pain. Layer by layer. And I'm down there, split. No, not there, not in the subway, stupid,' she laughed. 'Down in a pit. In a big black hole they dug for me specially. Sorry, this sounds like something out of a bad play, I know, and I'm spoiling your day out. So let's do something sensible to cheer ourselves up, like—'

We were interrupted by a middle-aged woman who recognised Amanda and greeted her rather effusively. In seconds she was transformed into a chattering, gossiping, friendly, superior hostess. For a moment she looked stunning, yes, her hair swinging as she moved about in animated conversation with the other woman, voice rising and laughing a lot. No trace of the melancholy she expressed talking to me.

As soon as we were alone again, she reverted to her former state. No, it was something new, a deliberate silence as we walked miles northward, punctuated by a few polite, trivial remarks. She rehearsed for me the names of the buildings we passed: Public Library, St Patrick's, Rockefeller Center, Presbyterian Church – perfunctorily like a boring city guide, without enthusiasm, simply not 'with it'. My own conversational sallies, discreet and impersonal to accommodate her mood, failed to rekindle our communication. An old black man dressed in a bright red jacket was selling red roses on the corner of 57th Street. On impulse I bought a rose for her, a little conscious of old-style chivalry that might not be all that well received in her present mood. But she accepted it graciously, with a half-smile and muttered thanks, walking beside me as a silent and detached companion. Silent but less grieving. I remembered that she lived not far from where we had got to, guessed that she would not invite me on that occasion and feared that we might part awkwardly, with no proper connection, creating nothing out of nothing, the classic 'end of the affair' before it had started. Yet I felt irrepressible waves of sympathy for her still, mixed with acute curiosity. For she had stirred me. That strange sobbing speech put an end to my planned neutrality. On impulse I suggested a walk in Central Park, not far away. She said it was getting chilly. Perhaps it was chilly, season of falling leaves. I do like the American word fall, so exact – falling, The Fall, fall for, fall flat, and other falls. As for the chill, I didn't feel it except as something that had emanated from her, an unpredicted whiff of the Arctic projected into the otherwise mellow city air. A brisk walk would revive her, I thought. So I hazarded some remark questioning her opinion about the weather (something neutral like 'are you sure?') and I offered her my coat. She rebuffed my remark and my offer. Then she suddenly turned on me, there in the street with passers-by staring, and said very loudly:

'What do you want from me?'

I said something meant to be reassuring, I wanted nothing. Whether she heard me or not, she went on to warn me not to repeat last year's horrible scene. Last year? When we were both in limbo? – in separate limbos, continents apart. I made a defensive gesture and tried to console her, moving a little closer but not all that close (I didn't touch her, I think). Then she shouted at me, 'Can't you see I'm old? Old!'

★

I woke with a kind of hangover, aching and blurred. I was just beginning to feel restored when I had a call from the reception telling me that there was a message for me. It was a handwritten scrawl, a scrap, from her:

> It's too much for me, sorry. Not today anyway, perhaps later in the week, but don't count on it. I'm frantically busy as you know. Plus the medical appointment. Enjoy the showroom and collect the catalogue. Greetings, Am.

The brief message hurt me. Beyond reason, for we had made no appointment. There had been a vague suggestion that we might go and see the Louis XVI showroom together, but, strictly speaking, there was nothing between us, as they say. Nevertheless, I was upset and confused. If everything had gone smoothly, there would be no need for me to write all this, trying to disentangle all that mess. What else can I call it?

'Too much' – what did that mean? Apart from the fact that I believe one can never have enough (at least that is what I always believed in my youth and I am trying to hold on to that belief, by hook or by crook) what was she complaining about? The climb to the top of the 107-floor tower or the long walk, the scene she made on parting? I had escorted her all the way, listened to her sympathetically, tried to comfort her. So what was going on in her shrunken head?

Sorry, I didn't mean that. I could see that she had suffered much in the past. But why take it out on me?

What was I to do? Fly out as planned? Then I would have carried with me the scars, so to speak, nothing crystallised, with the curse of unsatisfied curiosity. What was I curious about?

After our first meeting, after that totally unexpected kiss, I woke in the middle of the night with a spontaneous erection entirely directed at her, with no other figure surfacing, no supplementary fantasy. Not a big deal though relatively rare, not a biological miracle. Certainly not an adequate reason for postponing my departure. But then came my troubled thoughts about her, caring about her fragility: the stress lines under her greying eyes. Disturbing. A kind of dignity blending with something else – a pensive air, her words about someone else. As if she had used up all her energy and talent just to drag herself back from the abyss, to recover from some original catastrophe.

'Overwhelming dislocation', I have read somewhere about a woman years after some vile divorce.

But I didn't have to be caught up in all that – madness. Like banking with a bankrupt or going to sleep with an infected partner.

What then could I do for her? Nothing or little, less than little in that state. But her state might change, perhaps with my help. At least I could prove to her that she was not, decidedly not, old.

★

White on White by Malevich at MOMA – unparalleled quietness.

The satisfaction of complete solitude, the exact opposite of being with people, for example with Amanda. There is a kind of perfection in the fusion of two colourless colours without discord. I have heard that Malevich wanted just that: to get away from nature and human beings, get rid of hands, I think he said 'hands' but he might as well have said skull or penis. In the presence of that picture everything else ceases to matter, for the moment. There is no need for anything to happen, no need to be with anybody. Who needs adventure, if you can call meeting Amanda an adventure? No fear of loneliness or chaos. I could have stayed with *White on White* much longer; as it is I lingered till closing time.

Suddenly they formed a circle around me, in their long black cloaks, a tight circle of fanatical devotees leaving no room for escape. I had no idea what they wanted from me, but when I gave them some money – a few dollars – they chanted 'not enough!'. I gave them all I had on me but they kept pressing for more. What they really wanted, I later surmised, was to convert me into a true believer in the Christ of black people, the true Israel. They formed a circle around me and smiled. I didn't feel threatened but neither did I feel liberated. While all this was happening I could not help wondering how Amanda would have responded. Would she have been tempted? Felt sympathetic or harassed? Might she have screamed? I would not have let her down. The age of chivalry is dead but the urge to rescue a woman under attack will never die.

★

I decided to stay, even though nothing had happened, I hadn't heard from Amanda and my attempts to reach her had petered out like the sound of a faint whistle. All I got was her answerphone, a bored low-keyed voice. Unstimulated, I left no message, also afraid that there would be no reply. Still I felt impelled to postpone my flight by three days in the first instance. I was rewarded for this little act of trust in 'our' future by receiving a message the day after I had postponed my return journey. A very short message suggested a 'short walk' – i.e. she was giving me short time, sharp but short pain, a voice prompted.

We had breakfast together at a deli not far from her home,

talking casually. I could not summon much interest in her dissertation on bagels, muffins and pancakes, for her small talk sounded like a deliberate evasion of talking about herself or our time together. No feelings of any kind. Admittedly she smiled quite pleasantly when she came to the many varieties of fillings for a pancake. She had remained an altogether conscientious guide.

In the park I lost my sense of time again and I can only remember how she responded to the bronze storyteller. She looked up at the statue, at him, and away from me, in a curious, contemplative attitude. So I had time to take in her profile, for the first time, the resolute lines of the nose weakened by the hollows in her cheeks under a little girl's delicate ears. After minutes of silence she turned to me and said, casually at first:

'You know, Andersen was my favourite when I was a girl. Really. Read to by my older sister every night and later reading to myself late at night. I never get tired of it, not to this day. For some reason even the happy endings leave you sad because you remember all the horrible things that happened before. The snow and the ice, for example. Do you know *The Snow Queen*?'

I said yes insecurely, for I had only the vaguest recollection.

'Well then,' she said, 'perhaps you're prepared. Don't delude yourself, don't expect anything. Because, yes, there is always that splinter in the eye, so everything evil and ugly looks large. Do you remember? It is all the demon's work.

The mirror that crashed to the earth and burst into millions, billions of tiny pieces. Hardly as big as grains of sand. And then you get a speck in the eye, a splinter in the heart, a splinter that splits, keeps splitting everything you see and feel. And then the horrible lumps of ice in there.' She touched her breast and went silent. 'Horrible,' she muttered after a long pause.

'It's worse than jealousy, or the usual marital split. When you get kicked out of your bed you just crawl into another room and somehow, heaven knows how, manage to get a few hours' sleep. Next day you try and hold your head high ready to fight the monster again. But when you get kicked out of your own house, with nothing at all, nothing, you just can't do that any longer, I mean you can't collect yourself, there is no self. For a while you just wander about like a streetwalker or a bum. Like one of those schizophrenics let out of hospital, you've seen them, wrapped in a blanket, that woman in a filthy, tattered fur coat picking her breakfast from an ash can. Until they come and take you in against your will and then...

'I didn't want to talk about this! Why do you make me talk like this? Why do you keep asking all these questions? You are almost indecent, a voyeur, just like Patrick was. You get a kick out of watching a woman suffer, Patrick!

'Never mind. It doesn't matter. Anyway, in the story Gerda finds Kay, the lumps of ice are thawed out and the splinter of glass is washed away. And that's why it's called a fairy tale,' she cried.

★

While Amanda was talking the weather turned. A cold autumnal wind seemed to sweep us out of the park along with the dead leaves, yellow and sickly red. That time I really did feel the chill. The sudden change was eerie after a brief interval of Indian summer. We walked silently, perhaps talking between long pauses. I wanted to find some way to get closer to her. Interestingly, Amanda seemed to cheer up as the weather deteriorated. Her peels of laughter rang out in the thinning air. As soon as we reached the shops near Fifth Avenue, she announced that she was going to warm me up. She asked me to wait while she darted into a menswear store, and she returned carrying an elegant fawn-coloured cashmere scarf, which she proceeded to wrap around my neck attentively. There was something girlish in her gesture, especially the mixture of spontaneity and shyness. For she managed to drape the scarf around me from a distance, at least she put the cloth on me without touching my body at any point with her hands. A little later, when we reached her house, she stood outside the half-opened entrance door for a long time, lingering as if wanting to open the door to me and close it at the same time. Then she said something like not needing a houseboy, meant to sound funny (she laughed) but it struck me as a crude example of mood-smashing. After that there seemed to be a moment of tenderness when she stretched out both her arms towards me and put them on my shoulders, holding me there. We froze in this gesture, almost literally, for it was certainly getting colder. I told her that our position reminded me of a certain traditional dance where you hold your partner before the music strikes up.

'No music,' she said, 'but thanks for the trip.' I had the impression that she had shut the door after her with a bang.

★

Was Amanda playing games with me at this stage of her life? It seemed to me more likely, as I reflected on her situation, that she was genuinely fighting off something – not necessarily me, I could have been just a representative specimen. Through me she was beginning to punish someone, moderately but lethally.

I looked around me, and felt a sudden claustrophobia among all those tall buildings that made the street look narrow. The wind was sweeping the autumn leaves into heaps, more and more of them. Faces looked grimmer, bodies bent. The shop windows were full of useless objects, plastic furs, shoddy kitchen utensils, door handles, curtain hooks, and sex toys. From time to time a deafening noise. A fetid smell from nowhere. The harsh voice of a rap singer from beyond the next block. I lost my sense of direction. I remembered what a woman, a complete stranger, told me while waiting for a bus: 'Here everybody is lonely. And it is better to be lonely than violated. Especially if you are a woman who is no longer a chick. The guys you meet are useless – boys or geriatric cases, gays, pimps, weirdoes, drug addicts, gangsters or just married men out for a one-night stand.' That sounded like a bitter tall story. But suppose Amanda felt like that and was triggered by revulsion?

Privacy is a fine state but if everybody wants it at once loneliness is incurable. Everybody in a cell isolated for the sake of safety. Polite and bland on the surface, like Amanda when I met her, then unpredictably anxious and hostile.

The splendour and excitement of the city faded and I wanted to leave at once, but I was again held back by something like a feeling of obligation. This may sound completely ridiculous but I thought by now I owed Amanda – what? Rescue or succour, a word I never use normally. She was asking for something she could not ask for. She was hoping for something she thought was hopeless. I wondered whether I was not in love with her after all.

The ambiguities of her age had started to worry me as never before. If only one could achieve some clarity about the real nature of her body, biologically speaking, it would be easier to understand her mind or soul. It would then be easier to respond to whatever it was that she secretly desired, and so end this confusion. The point is that confusion gets painful if it goes on for any length of time and it is quite wrong – even corrupt – to get involved in another human being's disturbance. Unless there is relief, as in *The Snow Queen*.

★

Towards the end of the week I had another cryptic, handwritten message waiting for me at the hotel reception:

'Come if you still want to,' followed by a time and place only to be deciphered with difficulty.

As I walked into that sumptuous place (was it really the Algonquin?) I hardly recognised Amanda. I must have walked past her table twice at least, and then there she was, a glamorous young woman framed by the inmates of a retirement home, a geriatric reserve. Told to sit down, I hesitated, wondering what I was letting myself in for. Facing me sat an old lady whose deathly pale cheeks were covered with patches of bright rouge, the kind that a has-been movie star might have used once. Another woman had a heavy silver-topped stick laid across the table in front of her. Next to her a heavyweight woman seemed unable to sit up, was in fact half-bent over the table with a back that seemed permanently crooked. The fittest person in the group of strangers was a middle-aged man with a black and grey beard and wearing a French-type beret. He smiled at me knowingly and not very pleasantly.

'Meet my friends,' said Amanda, introducing them one by one with a happy-seeming but strained smile. I probably forgot their names instantly, no, the man was called Patrick, I remember. Frankly, I was once more preoccupied with my Amanda enigma but didn't wish to stay in that company. I tried to think of a good excuse for leaving at the earliest opportunity but could not – I was unable to leave. I was held back by some need to learn more, beyond curiosity. Every now and again I picked up a few fag ends of conversation but essentially I was watching Amanda, her reactions, her hands and her face, seemingly so calm and yet agitated for reasons not immediately clear. Patrick was holding forth almost without interruption, the old women around him nodding emphatically in grotesque agreement. I heard a few words about graffiti – on the subway trains, illegible scribble, meaningless, insane, not even gesture politics, not addressing anybody. Then some other topic, the sonorous voice was enjoying itself. Then he talked about something he had seen at the Met, now in a hushed voice as if marking a solemn occasion, until the whole class had to pay attention.

'Much better, better than Zeffirelli,' he said, 'because so simple. There are no baroque distractions, just a plain stage set and the singing. The best Leporello ever, the best catalogue aria. And you know why? Because of the wonderful transition from the mocking allegro to the lyrical andante. No, you can't guess! One minute just the hilarious catalogue of Don Giovanni's conquests, which everybody knows, you know – in Spain a thousand and three, repeat, repeat. It's absurd of course, the man has no soul. He might as well have laid them all with a machine gun all over Europe and in Turkey, but not in America, not yet.' (He paused, waiting for appreciation from us, the humble listeners.)

'So it doesn't matter who she is, what she does, where she is, or what she looks like, beautiful or ugly, young or old. OK? All this is wonderful stuff but not real, just a legend. Laugh and relax. You don't have to feel or you can feel really laid back. But then something absolutely incredible happens: this cynical guy Leporello completely changes his voice, gets soft and tender, kind of melancholy. He is telling the suffering wife – were they really married?, that's a question – how his master has managed it all, with extraordinary charm and a perfectly calculated approach to each type of woman. OK? And then he sings the catalogue, intoxicated by the praise of women, the praise appropriate for each type in turn, the tall one is majestic, the small one dainty, the older woman easily seduced, just to add to the list. And so on. And as he sings he gets right inside the mood, inside each woman, body and soul. Somehow he sings from within each seduction. Somehow the mocking servant catches the Don's passion like the plague, but he is better at it, I mean morally better because he sings with such compassion. Every now and then you catch a word, *la dolcezza*, *la piccina*, repeated and repeated by that mellow bass until you too experience *it*. I mean the passion together with the compassion, you catch it as you listen to that superb pimp. You may not understand the words at all but you know one thing, this guy is no longer boasting vulgarly about hooking thousands of skirts, his words, he is singing about the bottom line, he is singing about desire, how it is infinite, unstoppable and universal, this primal cry…'

Patrick was completely carried away, that was evident. I tried to remember as much as possible, even jotting down the gist of his speech afterwards. Unfortunately he managed to spoil the day, for Amanda and so for me, by a sudden provocation. Of course I did not immediately realise it was a provocation, only when I saw the effect he had on Amanda. I think what happened was a chain reaction. Our entertainer (I heard later that he had been a Broadway impresario in his prime) could see well enough that Amanda did not appreciate his performance. All the other women seemed to be listening with rapt attention but Amanda was frowning. So he suddenly said something I did not completely catch, for he spoke rapidly and angrily, but essentially he went on quite a bit about the same scene in *Don Giovanni*, stressing its ingenuity and how marvellous it was when that haunting Leporello aria gives the Don a chance to bolt. Just like that, he slips away invisibly while the music and the song last. You have to admire the villain.

'The coward!' said Amanda, the only word she spoke that morning.

Quietly, but somehow menacingly, Patrick then said that anyone would have to flee from a wife like Elvira. All she could do is to fill the void with lamentation, curses and cries for revenge. In reality she didn't give her husband a moment of peace, for she only wanted to pry into every hidden crack in his past, wanted to know what happened, where and with whom, in detail, find out all about him, possess his psyche, the key to all his previous relationships. So she was the villain, not he, because she was not going to let him keep his memory private and intact. I could sense an unpleasant undertone in all this but didn't pay much attention until I saw Amanda bite her lip. (I thought that was just an expression but here I saw it enacted.) Suddenly she stood up, picked up her glass filled with red wine and poured its contents down Patrick's open-necked shirt. She left the restaurant without a word.

I would have liked to be amused but my nervous system would not let me. I felt a sudden urge to follow her and comfort her, do whatever was required. But by the time I got out into the street I could see no trace of her in the crowd. I determined to follow her all the same, walking all the way to her home where I had never been. At the first crossing I stopped and gave my change to a blind beggar who, far from thanking me, called out in a high-pitched voice, 'O don't give me the pennies!' As I turned I bumped into a large black woman staggering about drunk or drugged or both. She spoke indistinctly but I guessed an offer of some indecent service 'in a quiet place'. I hadn't walked far before I felt very tired and changed my mind, thinking it would be counterproductive to see Amanda when I was incapacitated. So I went into a coffee shop, hoping to regain my energy. But the opposite happened, for the coffee did not stimulate and I was interrupted by an attractive if overdressed older woman who conjured up a luxurious residence on Long Island with swimming pool and sauna and, after a conversation about the trials of living in Manhattan, invited me on the spot. She said she knew instinctively that we had a lot in common, she knew my type. Of course I declined, pointing out that I was engaged. However, she insisted, gave me her address and phone number, asking me to call some time, any time. I thanked her but told her again, explicitly, that I was engaged. Later it struck me that there was something ridiculous in using that word so solemnly, as if I had committed myself in an old-world engagement. On the contrary, I was actually wondering that very moment how to put an end to this whole unpromising adventure with Amanda. Could anything come of it? Could I as much as see her? Instantly I was overcome by a new longing to see her, just to see, and perhaps find out…

I said goodbye to the coffee shop chatterer with unwonted abruptness. I had lost all desire to go on. I began to realise that I was not the man to rescue Amanda from whatever it was she was suffering.

★

I woke the following day still tired and once more thinking it was time to go. I even phoned to inquire about flights, but there was no flight on offer at just the right time and price. Then I woke for a second time: I acknowledged that I could not leave without at least saying goodbye to Amanda, a few words at least. I phoned several times in a matter of two hours and got the same mechanical, deadening answerphone. Finally she did answer. I naturally started in a low key even though my desire to see her was immediately renewed by the sound of her voice, muffled, hurt. Asked how she was, she just said, 'Bad!' A monosyllable and a slamming down of the phone. Perhaps it wasn't an angry slam, it may have been the lingering hangover from the painful case I had observed, followed by ordinary weariness.

I resumed walking around the blocks in the vicinity of my hotel without any sense of purpose. I naturally looked in the windows of every antique shop, pretending I was professionally engaged. I discovered a beautiful English clock, unmistakably William and Mary, with a mounted dial set with brass cherubs and a silver skeleton chapter ring in the spandrels, engraved with Roman numerals. I thought this would make a fitting birthday present for Amanda, remembering that she mentioned it was to be fairly soon but failing to remember the exact date. Anyway, I could just give it to her as an imaginative present, not a memento. However, the price was too high, not just for my budget but for any credibility – I mean that clock might have scared her off in her present state, she wouldn't have known how to respond, finding it embarrassing either to refuse or to accept and so spoiling the promise of a spontaneous moment.

Near the hotel I was stopped by a girl, she must have been a teenager, in the shortest mini-skirt and a charm dangling above her cleavage; another indecent proposal, and another refusal from me. This incident actually ruined the evening for it incongruously interrupted my pure desire for Amanda so that I was unable either to think about her with generous thoughts or call to the eye of the mind her body, which I had not yet seen.

★

I was asleep when the phone rang. It took me ages to focus on what she was saying. Unreal. Amanda's voice sounded thicker, the local twang in her accent shifting from the pleasant to the disconcerting. Her words tumbled out in an agitated torrent, disjointed. Something about going back to her lawyer – getting an injunction, sending in the bailiffs, justice at any cost. Any risk worth taking. Had waited three years, could not bring herself to sue, how could she when she could scarcely bring herself to lift a cup, feeling completely futile, the world totally blacked out as if hit by an asteroid, and nobody cared, not one friend.

'The main thing is, just to get my music back, and the violin. How can I live without my music? Patrick, are you listening? You're obviously not.'

I didn't feel like reminding her that I happened to be called Donald. I tried to say something reassuring but that made her even more agitated.

'You haven't got a clue, you are soft in the head,' she cried.

Then something about her son, how he couldn't care less, and Sarah itching to lay her hands on the only family porcelain she'd got, the bitch.

'Everybody is cheating, that's for sure, it's an epidemic. Nobody can be trusted. The few honest people are all dead or have Alzheimer's. A generation gone down the tubes. Rotten men, one after another, all they want is to penetrate you. And your husbands take all you have earned, everything you own, your letters and your music.'

I again tried to say something to show my, what? Sympathy, I suppose, mixed with exasperation and, when fully alert, a new sort of desire to run to her and calm her physically.

'Don't interrupt me, Patrick,' she called down the line, 'I know your tricks. It's all over between us, finished. All I want is my music!' and she slammed down the phone.

★

I arrived in fear and trembling, the old saying. Amanda ran down the stairs to greet me in the entrance hall of the condominium – laughing, shouting greetings merrily and giving me a hug, an effusive welcome. I no longer cared whether it was social or erotic at the time. Just to have gained entrance was enough, an unexpected achievement. After all, I had written her off, placed her in limbo with other discarded projects and women. The interval, the hopeless waiting, had been sheer misery, more or less repeating the anxious days I have recorded. I had been spending entire days mostly travelling on the subway (to the Bronx, for example) without really wanting to get anywhere, like a truant schoolboy who had discovered that there was nothing to do out there after all. Terrible freedom.

Through the tiny hall, I walked straight into her sitting room, sparsely furnished but in perfect taste with an authentic Empire sofa. How could she afford it? Or was it on loan? For a moment I saw ourselves seated there together, as on a love seat, but before as much as sitting down anywhere, Amanda excused herself: work, an urgent call, the accounts, also urgent –

'Won't be too long. Feel at home! There is a kettle and Earl Grey tea in the kitchen.'

End of excitement. She might as well have dumped me in a bucket of iced water. I know that there are men who get stimulated, impatient or angry but somehow functional while waiting, subjected to such trickeries of postponement. But I felt simply deflated by the prolonged waiting, wishing I could slouch out of that house without bye-byes. Instead, I studied the furnishings and I was particularly struck by the sofa, more precisely a *canapé* – the front legs carved as winged Egyptian monopodia with lion's paw feet. After a long while Amanda staged a re-entry. In a matter-of-fact manner she related to me the business just accomplished, which I paid little attention to. Then something, I can't remember what, reminded her of some other catastrophic episode from her second marriage – a child caught up in the conflict and damaged for life, she said. One day Patrick (or was it another name?) shot the German shepherd, her guard dog, with a gun he had suddenly produced out of nowhere, to punish and intimidate. Then she cried silently. I felt my sympathy flow in her direction, more strongly than ever before, but again I didn't know what to do or say. She had turned into a marble monument – *Woman Weeping*, after Rodin – out of reach and untouchable. Perhaps to break out of that emotional enclosure, she suddenly said:

'I saw you examine my sofa, and I'm glad you like it!' and she went on rehearsing the details, adding some I hadn't noticed but emphasising the lion's paw feet, as if she saw me as a buyer, perhaps an auctioneer. I was more intrigued than cross about what might have been just a conscious manoeuvre on her part, and when she smiled tenderly I again felt that she needed comforting. I drew a little nearer to her and carried on the conversation. While we were talking, Amanda became more and more animated yet palpably vulnerable, seductive in her own way again. She had shed her previous freezing-out position. Her head bent, her lustrous black hair allowed to fall more loosely than usual, with little or no make-up and natural-seeming eyelashes, the light in her eyes, a firm bosom indicated by the angle of her pullover – all suggested a kind of youth. Any speculation about her calendar age ceased to matter.

'So you see how it is, my friend,' she said.

I thought she was about to begin crying again. So I moved over to her corner on the sofa and gave her a light kiss – near the mouth but not on it.

She jumped up as if I had knifed her.

'What do you want from me? Idiot. Can't you see that I don't have a body? It is gone, decayed, putrid. I am covered in scars all over, look!'

She pulled up her pullover. I saw whitish, waxen breasts, shrivelled, purple nipples. A red sickle-shaped scar towards the abdomen.

'And what you don't see is worse, my womb and ovaries

surgically removed, my belly sliced open half a dozen times, my legs varicose, my vagina as dry as old leather – dry, dry, and totally silent. When I wake I smell like a skunk. Only a mad rapist would want to come near me. So keep away from my body, Patrick, if you don't want me to push you down those stairs again.'

She sobbed, but not for long. She switched to a calm and dignified tone: 'I am sorry to disappoint you but a little perception might have saved us this disgrace.'

I muttered something, wanting to explain…

'It's no use,' she interrupted, 'you must realise that this is the end of our friendship.' And she handed me my overcoat without another word, and without any other gesture.

IV

WIDOW

It was getting dark and cold when I reached the gates of the cemetery and found myself locked in, a strong chain reinforcing the iron gates, a few minutes after closing time. It seemed incredible that any gatekeeper should take the risk – was it not a crime? – to let a live human being be stranded there for a long winter night among over fifty-thousand graves. Uncanny. So many neglected graves, untended for decades, the stones mouldering or aslant in the muddy earth. The ground itself was dug up in many places, as if an army of moles had been at work heaving up irregular mounds. There was nothing to be afraid of, I thought, sooner or later they will release me. I rattled the gate loudly and shouted something to attract attention. An eerie silence followed, so I just stood there getting colder, trying to repress my more morbid thoughts.

'This is formidable,' a voice spoke behind me, 'a scandal,' she said.

I turned and saw an ageless woman in a tight-folded dark overcoat, not black, I think, but my memory is blurred. My first response was relief, ah, another human being, together we can make more noise and finally get attention. I must have said something encouraging to cheer us up, the strange woman and myself. Whatever I said had the wrong effect, however, for the woman burst into tears and, when I made another friendly remark, started sobbing. She said something incomprehensible. Then I could just make out isolated words: 'the worst visit...I could not speak to him...I was dumb...the first time ever nothing to say to him... paralysis...the final death.'

★

By the time we sat down in a sober-seeming wine bar, my new companion was composed. She introduced herself as Gisele and I guessed from her slight accent and one or two other signs that she had a French background. She said nothing, at first, about the emotion that had engulfed her at our first encounter. Instead she talked about a private pupil who was linguistically gifted but tiresome. Then, prompted by some remark – was it a casual naming of God, as in 'Oh, God, I forgot'? – she lowered her voice to an intense whisper as she leaned across the table almost touching me:

'After his first massive heart attack, when everybody thought he must die, he had a vision. He had seen the face of God, and talked to me every day, calmly, clearly, as we talk about any experience, something nobody can possibly question. For it is impossible to say to somebody who talks to you about his joy, "Oh no, you are mistaken, there is no such thing as joy in this world!" So he talked to me every time I sat by his bedside, you know, every day for weeks, about beautiful things brought back from a world beyond this one, about the trust between us which was like the force of love. He said it was the foundation of the universe. He said death did not matter, because we were immersed in the element of love. He said that separation was not real because love is not like the physical heart, if *it* stops, everything else stops, perhaps astrophysics, the whole cosmos. He said that he had never felt better in his life than in his terminal illness, that it was a gift and when the time comes it will be just like slipping from one dark room into another at night, when you don't turn on the light so as not to wake up the others. He was not leaving me. But for a while – he never said how long – he wanted me to visit him daily, and to concentrate by his grave, that's the word he used, concentrate and communicate. That would make it easier for him to…to reach me. Then no obstacle or accident could prevent him, he would respond. He even joked that it was like spiritual e-mail, an immediate message and instant reply. One day he said…'

She broke off. This time her eyes were dry and shining, seemingly with pleasure. After long silence, for I had no idea how to answer, she said in a normal voice but for some reason with her French accent and idiom more pronounced: 'You see now the impossibility of doing anything else than visit the cemetery. Every day. And now perhaps you will begin to comprehend my situation.'

I felt a wave of sympathy but remained baffled. I must have filled in the next silence with some vague remarks about mortality, trying not to sound too sceptical about the afterlife. For though she could not convert me to her faith, she was beginning to convert me to herself. Her quiet voice had a fine resonance. Her hand gestures kept sending wordless messages, friendly ones. When we finally moved out into the street again, I could not help noticing her slender figure. She stepped out with a youthful spring though she must have been in her late forties. When she bent down to pick up a dropped key, I felt a moment of attraction, a passing moment. I would have felt embarrassed if not guilty if that attraction had lasted longer than a moment, given the circumstances of our meeting, her sorrow, and my fresh determination to give up adventure.

★

Less than two weeks later I had a short letter from her. It stated, with almost cold formality, how comforting she had found it to engage in conversation with me when we met by chance, making no reference whatever to the wonder of the occasion, or to her emotion at the time. She added a sentence inviting me to a modest *soirée* at her little apartment – her words – warning me not to expect anything special and to bring nothing except myself. This elevated tone was decked out with a funny little doodle in the corner of the letter making me look like Asterix scratching his head, I have no idea why. I was surprised by this invitation. Somehow I didn't expect a woman in mourning to go in for parties, nor to take an initiative in my direction. After all, I did tell her when we met that I was a busy man and a frequent traveller – true, but I must have said this to forestall, yes, any further meeting in the near future, so as not to risk further complexities.

By the time I got to her place, a roomful of people were engaged in merry chatter, drinks were being poured and an older man, who turned out to be her father-in-law, was in the middle of a story from his war experiences in the army. Something about being locked into a barn with the milking cows during the whole battle. Everybody seemed to find that funny except me. After a stilted round of introductions, I was given a glass of Sauterne with *petits fours* before being virtually abandoned in a corner of the room with the anecdotal father-in-law.

Across the room Gisele looked disturbingly attractive, in a short, sleeveless, black dress with a loose wrap around otherwise bare shoulders. Showing too much flesh, my mother would have said, after all she was still in mourning. Also, she was wearing a pendant that kept swinging over her cleavage when she moved or bent down, and I could hear her hoots of high-pitched laughter. It did not sound merry. Under strongly marked dark eyebrows the protruding cheekbones looked quite sensual as they caught the light. But I could see the skull, the sockets.

When she sat down on the sofa, she threw her head back in an elegant position which looked to me somehow studied, playing off her stylishness like a virtuoso performer. And her voice sounded luscious yet menacing.

She took me on a sort of guided tour around her flat, leaving the guests to entertain themselves. She allowed me a glimpse of her bedroom before she switched off the light that she had only just switched on. A disturbing effect. I had seen enough to see that one wall was covered with photographs, mostly portraits of the same man in various poses – in hat and coat, in a dinner jacket, wearing nothing on a beach – the same face, not young but sharp-edged and virile, bearded, unsmiling, staring, obviously scrutinising her every movement, jumping out of the frame. Small-size variants of these photos were propped up on her dressing table and I glimpsed a miniature version of the same face on the bedside table. When the light went off she said with a kind of piety, 'We must leave at once.'

Minutes later we were in the kitchen, in a state of upheaval with piles of dirty dishes and plates all over the place, on tables and working spaces: the residue of the party still in progress. She picked up a half-empty bottle of white wine and poured out two glasses, accompanied by slurred words. I realised that she was getting tipsy but she seemed to remain in control. Whilst I refused the wine she greedily poured another glassful down her throat. Suddenly she reached for a bowl of fruit and offered it to me; to please her rather than wanting the fruit, I took a small bunch of red grapes. Gisele did exactly the same as if copying me and then, laughing immoderately, pushed a grape between my lips. When I opened my mouth to thank her she laughed louder still and repeated the gesture with compound interest: she came closer and meticulously pushed another grape, this time straight from her mouth into my mouth, with her tongue, transferring a load of wetness. I hardly had time to swallow before I felt her kiss, a light kiss followed by a passionate one as she leaned against the sink and drew me into her breasts.

'What about the guests?' I heard myself say.

Gisele shouted something abusive. Why did she get so angry? She looked as if she was going to hurl some crockery at me, the classic domestic act I had read about somewhere. Fortunately nothing quite as vulgar happened, she just pleaded tearfully:

'Can't you see that I want to forget? Imbecile!'

After that she sounded like one of those ill-edited tape recordings where essential sections in someone's speech are inaudible for minutes. I had no idea what exactly she was trying to say but I suspect that just about every word she launched at me in that scene was offensive.

The party was lively enough but, with Gisele out of reach, boring. I watched her getting animated with others and wondered whether she was making a forced effort to titillate them. But she could not have faked the glow on her cheekbones. The next thing I remember is saying goodbye to her in the half-dark hall, standing in front of an alcove full of overcoats, boots and shoes. She again came close to me, so close that I thought she was going to trap me in that corner. Instead she pulled herself up and addressed me in a solemn if not reproachful tone:

'My trouble with you is that you are not quite authentic. Perhaps almost but not totally. Something is missing, a deficit. And…there is another…. . I can trust the other more. I shall tell you about him…if there is a next time. I am very intuitive, and I know…you don't feel what I feel, my friend. That all nature is corrupt. That death is experienced every day. You don't read Pascal and so, my dear Don, I permit myself to call you so, you fail to recognise the desert in life, when there is only rottenness, misery, error, loneliness, despair and death. But I wish you a very good night.'

I felt that she was doing her best to be sincere but, as I was leaving, I had a distinct vision of Gisele giving me a cue for a dignified stage exit, to fit into her scene. Back in my flat I had a poor night with confusing dreams. She came to me with a distorted face, a young girl staring with owlish eyes. She forced me to write down a list of my crimes – she said I was too stupid to know what they were and she kept repeating and repeating certain words: liar, libertine, libidinous. When I woke up I jotted down what little I remembered, laughing to myself at the thought that she had forgotten to add necrophiliac.

★

What did she want, what did this woman really want? The

question baffled me even more after her second, improvised, invitation. We met by chance in the West End on a cold winter afternoon, and talked casually; I was determined to carry on with my town errands. Suddenly she turned round and planted a light kiss on my lips. 'Come for supper tonight if you are free,' she said, with a furtive smile, waved me off with her gloved hand, and was gone.

I felt restless and hot in the cold air, transformed. Remnants of hoar frost marked the verges of grass in the park when I started on my vigorous walk, a head-clearing exercise as if trying to make a difficult business decision. Apprehension and desire were tossing a coin, so to speak. I decided to opt for a compromise: make a phone call, say a few encouraging things, celebrate our chance meeting, tell her what she perhaps wanted to hear – how exciting it was to meet by chance, how much better than making an arrangement, writing a letter, making a phone call, et cetera; I would stress the importance of spontaneity again. No, you can't rehearse spontaneity, but make her feel cared for and wanted. Add: 'I must inspect a bureau, sorry, it is overdue.' That would be the best strategy, I had convinced myself.

In any case, I argued, the natural impulse had already been sapped, desire was cooling; she had given me far too much time for reflection. Hours! If she had really wanted to improvise she should have done so convincingly and made sure we acted impulsively, instantly. Why didn't she encourage me, spur me on? Some ambivalence on her part, no doubt. Other women knew exactly what to do, how to sustain temptation, not to let it sag or flag. But to leave such a gaping gap of time was intolerable. The empty hours stretched between wanting and not wanting until the latter came uppermost, in a kind of death wish. Had she intended that?

In the end I did what she had asked me to do and presented myself, much later than seven, her customary time for dinner. I delayed because I was afraid. What was her next move going to be? What strategy?

Gisele greeted me strangely, with a grave, almost ceremonious politeness while smiling profusely. She led me straight into her living room, which also looked stranger than when I saw it as a guest at her party not so long ago. It looked like an empty waiting room. Ah, I thought, all those people had gone, thank goodness. But no, there was something else, something quite disturbing – the furniture must have been shifted, several items removed and only one item of interest left: an oakwood chest, probably Jacobean, certainly early seventeenth-century English. A pile of photograph albums, each held together by a thick black ribbon, were placed on top of the chest so that one did not feel like inspecting them. Everything else was poor stuff, an odd mixture of Ikea and *bric-à-brac* from Camden Town. Her much-mourned husband had left her without means, I thought. So here was a poor woman creating a little luxury world out of airy nothing. But there was something else that I only noticed after she had made me sit down on a three-seater sofa (covered with what looked liked a worn William Morris curtain) at a distance too self-consciously insisted on by her. It was the strangeness of the light: bright yet mellow, illuminating our area and leaving the rest of the room half-buried in shadows. A spotlight lit up yet another portrait of her deceased husband.

Her face seemed to shine amid the dark shadows as if she had been posing for a late Victorian fashion photographer. A noble forehead, but the high cheekbones protruded and looked sensual, as before. Dressed in a black blouse with a white collar, demure, almost puritanical, while the tight-fitting short sleeves gave prominence to the shape of her beautiful arms. Subdued beams of light converged on the bare skin of her neck, elongated as if stretched, making her look taller than her actual height, a simple optical illusion. Where have I seen this before? Perhaps in a de la Tour painting. Only then did I realise that we were immersed in candlelight. I kept still, for it would have been inappropriate, sacrilegious – to use an antique word – to break the silence or to make any crude gesture in her direction.

In that still moment I was moved by everything about her and felt impelled to move towards her.

She got up then and lighted the candles in the candelabra on the dining table and also a set of tall red candles in wall-lights or sconces. I gathered that I had to wait until the dinner was ready, but then some thought stopped her and she just stood there as a statue – one of those wrapped figures standing immobile by the kerbside until someone gives her a coin. She gave me a curious look that made me feel quite uncomfortable, with anxious desire.

'I know what you are thinking but it's not true,' she said.

That sounded cryptic and I dared not question her. In any case, she mercifully ended her scrutiny of my face – and my motives? – and treated me to a childhood memory.

'It isn't so very special, you know, all these candles, not for me. I grew up with candles, in our house always, every night, especially in winter. And outside my home too, and I do not mean the church. We always went out late, when it was pitch dark, especially the night before All Saints, and then suddenly we saw that great field of lights in the cemetery, a million candles lit for the dead. I remember thinking, I was only seven, how the dead needed the light. To see the lights flicker over the dark graves, that was the one essential thing. And to get close. Even the smell was good – a strange smell which always comes back in unexpected moments. The air was full of whispering but not one audible word. Maman would not allow a long stay. So back home quickly, to bed after a bath and hot chocolate. One slept perfectly then. I mean, after such a visit one never had nightmares, never. And in the morning the people in the streets looked better, kinder somehow.'

She had been speaking softly but expressively, with fine body language, head bent. Again she gave me a searching look, and again it was impossible to say or do anything. I was immobilised just when I had the strongest feelings towards her. When the grip of the moment began to loosen, I tried to approach her and say something, a hint of what I felt and desired without sounding sentimental, but she interrupted my thoughts:

'So you see that's why, perhaps you have guessed already, I think of him so intensely just tonight. It is remembrance. We all need that every day.'

★

I couldn't have heard the knock. Lying on my sickbed, I got absorbed in reading. In any case, I had not been expecting anyone. Five o'clock in the afternoon was not a visiting hour, and how on earth did she manage to make her way up to the third floor and so to the end of that endless corridor, without as much as being challenged? And what did she want from me, what? What was she about to inflict on me? After such a long absence. Just when my greatest need was rest, convalescence medically prescribed. For the sake of peace I'd chosen a room without telephone and television, refused newspapers, ate most of my meals alone, told my friends not to visit for at least two weeks (told her nothing – we had been out of touch when I became ill) and I kept indoors as much as possible, only going out for health walks in the still wintry gardens of the convalescence home. Under the circumstances nothing could be worse for me than to be upset again.

She brought me red roses and red grapes. I wondered whether she was trying to remind me of our grape scene, in bad taste under the circumstances. Anyway, it was impossible to refuse her gift but also impossible to accept it with good grace. Neither could I greet her with any enthusiasm, at best with cool formality. I think I saw her as Charlotte Corday about to lift her murderous knife above Marat in his medicinal bath.

Meanwhile she just stood there, silently and patiently, in the middle of the small room, furnished only with a bed, a wardrobe and a coffee table. There was something humble in her posture, slightly bent, yet she smiled radiantly when she looked at me, looking younger and more vigorous, more healthy than I remembered, with an air of self-assurance as if she knew exactly what she was going to say and do to me.

After a while she started talking in a grave yet gentle voice, embarking on a kind of morale-boosting chat with an experienced bedside manner – how well I looked, how pleased she was *it* was not more serious, she knew a lot about the human heart, inevitably, recovery virtually guaranteed, Spring was coming, then perhaps a trip to Paris. Together?

She sat down on the edge of my bed. Admittedly there was only one chair in the room and that was covered with my clothes, for I preferred to stay in bed in my pyjamas although that was no longer a requirement. I still think Gisele tried her best to please me, she must have expected me to be pleased. She adopted a caring attitude and offered to read to me from a paperback anthology of love poetry she had brought with her. Not in good taste, I thought, and declined.

That turned out to be a mistake for then there was no option left except talking or doing something; there seemed to be no other way in her repertoire. She kept making rather fine, soothing remarks, treating me as an interesting patient, I couldn't help observing, before she reached out for me through a slit between the buttons – without encouragement. She started stroking my chest gently without stopping until she must have felt me flinch. She kept fiddling with the hair on my chest, mumbling something about how fur tended to turn her on, then she stroked one of my nipples, pointing out that a man's nipples were absolutely useless anatomically except, she said laughing immoderately, for making a man rise. And it is true that I was beginning to enjoy her treatment somewhat, perhaps visibly, for she was emboldened. All the while she said little, resorting to murmurs and mumbles. This went on. I let her go on, half-fascinated, half-repelled. I really expected her to come to her senses and stop spontaneously, without my having to take defensive action. But she did not stop, she moved her hands further down, slowly and rhythmically. Then she sat on me. She accomplished this feat so lightly that I didn't notice her move, only the result.

There began within me then one of those ageless battles between body and spirit in which there is no winner – the body rising, if not quite fully, and the spirit, aided by ordinary common sense together with the demands of hygiene, resisting inadequately. She sat on my tummy, managing a degree of weightlessness that must have come from practice for it did not have the air of an instinctive position. In the end my justified hypochondria won the day. As I felt my pulse rise, my heart audibly banging, a sharp angina-like pain recurring, with memory of the pain that had landed me in intensive care in the first place only three weeks earlier, I naturally shouted out: 'Stop that!' My shout must have been unconvincing for she kept molesting me, albeit less recklessly. I plainly told her that if I consented to her desire I would die.

'Nonsense,' she said, with amazing cheek, 'I really do know more about these things than you. From previous experience.'

She gave up in the end, but only when she had satisfied herself that my pain was not faked. After she had climbed off my bed she squatted on the floor, looking at me with an expression suggesting reproach rather than regret. My only defence was to repeat the sheer facts of my condition, with some exact details from my medical report specifically ruling out sudden movement or violent exertion. Only then did she express a slight sense of remorse, not exactly apologising but muttering something about how all she wanted was a smile, followed by something healthy and uplifting to restore both of us, with closeness and beauty. Then she started philosophising about deferred hope, giving me a large chunk of Greek mythology, mostly Tantalus, no doubt intended to calm me down.

'It's no use, no use,' she said after a while, sounding defeated.

After that she seemed to have lost her confidence and began to plead for some understanding: deprived and solitary since the death of her husband, when she didn't, couldn't want anything, not even a minimal life. She asked me not to be absolutely insensible to suffering…and not to be typically patriarchal…dismissing women of a certain age, after the menopause to be precise. It was a caricature to think of such a woman as no longer a woman, no more childbirth therefore no more anything, no looks, figure, ability, spirit, sex. A mature woman could be more free and fulfilled, no need for hormone replacement therapy. The spirit was more important than the body, but that did not mean one was obliged to spend the rest of life in a nunnery…

She went on like this for quite a while, using odd words with a more than usually marked French accent so that I could only follow what she was saying by hard concentration. And I don't suppose I heard half of it, probably missed her subtler points. But I do remember that she worked herself up into a kind of fury, which seemed unreasonable at the time. After all, was she not scolding an invalid, I asked myself, as my chest began to hurt again.

Then she suddenly changed her tune. I think after I had put my hand on my heart to test the pain, her attitude changed utterly.

'Sorry, sorry, I am really sorry. This is terrible and I am terrible, like that poor mad woman Phèdre with her *"Vénus tout entière á sa proie attachée"*. Clinging. You have opened my eyes,' she said crying, 'to my own guilt. That will now be a burden, perhaps for the rest of life. Perhaps *he* died because I wanted to console him…with my love. Perhaps I killed him!'

I said nothing. I wanted to say something consoling but couldn't. Deeply embarrassed I looked away, to give her time to regain her composure. When I looked up the room was empty.

★

I must admit that on our arrival in Paris I couldn't help asking: Why here? Why now? Why with her? And why emptiness rather than wonder, when one might have expected a little joy at long last? What was the matter with Gisele, still or again? After all, the journey had been her own idea, a long-cherished desire. And it was a perfect journey, first-class Eurostar with dinner, then encamping in a good little hotel in Saint-Germain, she my guest, for the cousin or friend who had invited us didn't materialise after all and she had no money. Who was this friend anyway, she or he, why so secretive? Ah well, a phantom or an impostor.

Despite Gisele's sulky mood, I was almost thrilled in the first hour of arrival. The Gare du Nord after many years, standing in the fast-moving taxi queue, giving directions in my rusty French, driving over the Seine, the lights on the bridge, a glimpse of the river and the *quais*, the checking-in ceremony by Madame who pretended to remember me, in time for a night walk along the riverside (or so I had hoped to begin with), the smell of coffee and garlic, the faded but not too faded curtains, finding our rooms in separate wings. Was that an accident or a trick? Hadn't I asked for adjoining rooms? Anyway, I felt perhaps thirty years younger, reliving my first visit, first love, first intoxication, refusing the tarts and Folies Bergères, going for the higher pleasures, out to Versailles and Chartres, burgeoning interest in antique furniture, late Picasso and Jean Jouvet as Tartuffe, together with the new light verse of Jacques Prévert:

Je suis comme je suis
Je suis faite comme ça...

J'aime celui qui m'aime

And the company! Kindred spirits, still under the long shadow of the war. Dancing in a puddle, getting lost on the metro, every day some new exhilaration. A kind of communion. A kind of euphoria in the intervals of dejection. 'Bliss was it to be alive then but to be young was *almost* heaven.' Of course I got totally broke, tried to borrow the return fare from the British Embassy, only to be brusquely rebuffed, developed such a fever at the youth hostel that I wrote a farewell letter on a crumpled sheet of squared paper, announcing my death.

All this and much more passed through my mind before I turned round and saw her pale, still sulky face. What's the matter, I wondered again but didn't ask. Later Gisele mumbled something about feeling very, very tired (or did she say 'weary'?) and sick, the sick word added as an afterthought, in a false-seeming faint voice. I felt some sympathy but was secretly dissecting her. Why, for example, couldn't she raise a smile? One faint smile at least. Some physiological handicap or merely self-mutilation of spirit? Even pretending might have been better at such a strategic time, our first bedtime. Was she disappointed in advance, so to speak? And, if she was feeling so feeble, how could she run up the stairs to her room with such alacrity, like a schoolgirl.

I managed to spend the remaining two and half hours before midnight wading through my old Michelin guide to refresh my memory of the city and plan our all too short stay, an exercise that gave me more satisfaction than a walk with Gisele in her present state would have done, just as once the Lion Gate of Mycene glimpsed in a travel brochure gave me more delight than the site itself, years later, visited in the company of a competent Greek archaeologist.

★

I started the following day determined to eliminate all expectations. This was wise because over breakfast Gisele had the air of a bored bourgeoise who had been married to me for at least twenty-five years, conspicuously attentive to the waiter and demonstratively indifferent to my presence. She was feeling better, she said, keen to go shopping on her own, if possible track down her friend (the one who let us down with the accommodation) and perhaps go out to the Père-Lachaise Cemetery where she needed solitude, evidently. After some awkward fencing with various alternatives for the day, we agreed to meet again after six. She accepted my suggestion that we should then go to the evening concert at Sainte-Chapelle. Before parting she did manage the smile I had been missing and, for a brief interval of time, she was restored into a delightful travel companion and a desirable woman.

Cherishing her parting image, I spent the rest of the day more or less agreeably. I paid a duty visit to the Musée des Arts Décoratifs, concentrating, on this occasion, on a few fine Boulle commodes, *en contrepartie* tortoiseshell and steel. But this errand proved to be less rewarding than usual, as I felt no sense of urgency, either professionally or personally. So I decided to postpone calling on my favourite furniture dealer in the rue du Faubourg St-Honoré. After a while I felt worse than lonely, re-experiencing the deadly flatness of bedtime last night, induced by Gisele's empty gestures. I was afraid that the whole expensive expedition might turn out to be sheer waste. Neither solitude nor contact, despite a growing desire to achieve contact.

It was in such a state that I walked over to the galleries of French painting in the Louvre. After acres of tedious historical pictures I was startled to see again Watteau's *Embarcation on the Isle of Venus*, a picture I considered frivolous in my arrogant youth. Now it seemed to be painfully beautiful, despite the obvious Rococo artifice, the little party of would-be lovers almost dwarfed by the menacingly enchanted landscape. A sad vision of make-believe happiness, frozen movement. And the act of arrival was a departure. You can only see the back of the man in the centre of the picture as he seems to turn towards a lady who does not meet his gaze. I remembered that Watteau was a sick man who died of consumption at an early age. Perhaps it was his awareness of the fragility of beauty which gave to his art that intensity.

It seemed a long day on my own, despite all that splendour around me but I was still reluctant to admit to myself that I was missing Gisele. My first reaction was to resent her absence. After all it was she, not I, who had been making plans, mapping out shared itineraries for each day, reminiscing and indulging in nostalgia. By late afternoon I felt tired enough to walk back to our hotel to make sure to be fresh and well-prepared for our evening adventure. On my way I stopped at the Pont-Neuf and discovered the tip of the island. Discovered is the word, for though I must have passed the place on previous visits, this time I saw it in sharp focus for the first time. Down by the river, down the steps behind the statue of Henri IV, a magnificent panorama in total stillness. There was nobody else there at the time. But the perfect moment was broken by further disturbing thoughts of Gisele – was it not betrayal? Perhaps it would all turn out well in the end. That same place, it occurred to me, could provide a setting for our reunion: I would guide her to the place, show its beauty to her, regain our lost closeness. But a glance at my guidebook seemed to mock that prospect for it earnestly informed me that the name of the place, Square du Vert-Galant, derives from the nickname given to Henri IV, alluding to his reputation as an amorous gentleman despite his age. (The guide ended the sentence with an exclamation mark, which I judged to be completely superfluous.)

The silence was interrupted by a group of schoolchildren, hardly children for some of them were visibly a couple of years past puberty, certainly the girls but some of the boys too, chattering loudly and moving about with a degree of self-conscious swagger or self-display but quite disciplined in a way. They scattered into groups of two or three near the embankment and immediately began sketching aspects of the view. I watched them for minutes. I was about to resume my walk when I caught sight of a slim, dark-haired girl, hair cascading below her shoulders, head bent over her sketchbook. She was kneeling, gracefully balanced, sketching the river scene – just a collage of colours to be seen, seemingly abstract with a suggestion of water and stonework within an elliptical design. She was wearing an anorak open in front, and when she turned round she exposed an astonishing expanse of white skin, her slender long neck giving way to naked shoulders. She remained quite still for a long time, only her fingers moving with her crayon in assured artistic measure. Suddenly she turned round again: dark, luminous, alert eyes under dark eyebrows in a pale oval face, no make-up of any kind. She smiled a generous smile and waved, as if to me. Immediately she turned away and nudged the girl sitting nearest to her, perhaps to make it appear that the smile and the wave was not, after all, directed at anyone. Too late. I have had eye contact with her for a fraction of a second, that I am sure of, and she must have been conscious of the contact, she must have felt it in some miniscule way, and it no longer mattered to what extent and for how long. It was irrevocable and worth a journey, as the guidebook says, but that sounds vulgar, for such a meeting is – words fail – beyond a journey. It can only be defined, if at all, in negatives – it has *not* brought delay, hesitation, duplicity, conflict, betrayal, abuse of beauty or torture. Unlike all those other occasions, with their ridiculous waste of time! All I needed, then, was a glimpse, a surprise, a moment of wonder without caring about any possible continuity in actual experience.

★

I waited and waited outside Sainte-Chapelle with growing impatience and anxiety. I had not anticipated such a crowd at the entrance and perhaps I simply failed to spot Gisele among so many people, despite her above average height. First I couldn't remember what she had been wearing in the morning and then, in near panic, I couldn't remember what she looked like. Her image got blurred or other faces surfaced as in a photograph album where some pictures had slipped from their corners and formed a human collage. I had seen too many images, it was time to jettison…. Then the feeling crept on me that I had simply been stood up, she was cavorting with her nameless friend, no doubt her lover. Perhaps not. Perhaps held back by a tombstone in that famous cemetery. In my worry about her I became much less sympathetic towards death. Wasn't her preoccupation with the dead becoming anti-life, or anti-me? Just an act? Let the dead bury the dead, I quoted.

In the end she did turn up, after I had given her up in a black mood of rejection. She arrived in the last possible minute, when the doors of the great chapel were about to be shut, out of breath and flushed; she said nothing – not 'sorry', not greeting me – just a nod in my direction suggesting take me or leave me, who cares what goes on in your little mind. There was a delay of perhaps two minutes between being seated and the tremendous moment when the choir began to sing the Requiem to the sounds of the organ. Gisele sat still and speechless but leaning towards me, I imagined. Not likely, but it seemed natural to expect at least some friendly gesture in that magnificent place.

What was going on in her mind? What was she thinking, feeling? Was she concentrating at all? Did she *see* the unparalleled stained glass? The revolutionary texture of the glaziers had completely replaced the stonework of walls and columns. The gradually darkening blue light in the glass kept out the outer darkness of the approaching night. It looked as if the strange illumination would never cease but when, in the middle of the concert, I looked up, the soaring vertical windows had gone completely dark. But did Gisele see it, did she see anything at all? I noticed a stiffness in her shoulders, perhaps from too much walking but communicating a general stiffness of spirit.

Did she hear the music at all? Surely that strange Requiem could not leave her cold. It is impossible to describe music from memory. The dominant mood was quiet yet exalted, a body was laid to rest without lamentation. No pomp, no opera. Anguish without show. At times a few isolated Latin words could be heard – *lux* – *morte* – from what sounded like a Gregorian chant. An immense sadness. I think Duruflé's Requiem would have moved me at any time, but hearing it in this place and this company brought a kind of ecstasy. My sympathy towards Gisele returned, redoubled, cancelling my earlier discontent. Surely she could not remain immune to such a perfect moment. Her grief would be renewed and turn into love, or at least sympathy... . I resolved not to say anything about my feelings when the concert was over. I just waited to see what might happen between us under the influence of that music.

We walked silently towards the Seine. Was that a smile? I tried to move closer to her but, on the point of taking her arm, I felt a tug in the opposite direction. So she again wanted to move away from me, creating a gap. What was going on? Had she been disappointed by the music? Was she feeling unwell physically again? Still sulking? She remained impenetrable.

After a while I brought up the idea of a walk to the river,

to the tip of the island I had discovered earlier in the day, trying to make it sound irresistible. It was no longer cold; winter was almost over or could be declared to be over. The air was soft and encouraging. Gisele refused my invitation but I thought there was some ambivalence, some coyness in her refusal, for I detected the trace of a smile and interpreted her polite 'no thanks' as provisional acceptance. So I repeated my offer, moved closer and touched her arm lightly for emphasis. At that she flung her whole body into reverse, so to speak, upsetting my balance in every sense of the word.

We could do nothing after that except start walking back to the hotel. She walked at such a pace that I could hardly keep up with her, in fact lagged behind her. But still I thought she was being playful, moody but not hostile. It was exciting to speed up and walk beside her again and anticipate a scene of reunion. Back in the hotel we sat down on a sort of love seat just behind the lobby, a public place with people crossing and staring. Gisele was silent. I naturally took this as a sign that she was, after all, deeply moved by the requiem and experiencing some kind of catharsis. There was no need to talk. At the same time her body language seemed more relaxed indoors: she sat back languidly, crossed her legs, took off her cardigan, revealing bare arms almost to the armpits, and she no longer tried to avoid my gaze. For a fraction of a second she looked me straight in the eyes, long enough to disturb.

Then she got excited about something, I think while she

was telling me the story of her camel ride, somewhere in the North African desert, with a young Arab who guided her, adored her, kissed her and…she didn't complete the story. Was that all? Her talking points became more personal – something I had been missing during our three days in Paris. She revealed for the first time that she was not a Parisian after all, had no particular fondness for Paris and had no desire to 'return' as she had led me believe. She was born and bred in Auvergne and she tried to regale me with its volcanic scenery, a sort of lunar landscape with craters, and the fine Romanesque churches of the region. She even sang a folk song about the lads who didn't feel like dancing:

Il ne fallait pas venir
Si vous ne vouliez pas danser

Don't come if you don't want to dance with me, I roughly interpreted, and I took this as an invitation to a dance, implicit and coded but still…. . Quite simply, she had become delightful again. So I moved closer to her, as far as the public place allowed. 'Don't push!' she said, and I obediently moved back an inch or two on the seat wondering whether she really meant it. Soon she stood up declaring that she felt really sleepy (it was getting near midnight, it is true). She stopped on the second stair leading to her room and said goodnight quietly, so softly that a memory-shot instantly recalled the way she used to be, how forthcoming, and how I had retreated from her, more than once, on account of bad timing. Now the time seemed more propitious. I moved up and touched her upper arm minimally before she could continue mounting those stairs (quite a distance from mine, as already observed). I was standing two steps under her, a positional disadvantage which she instantly found a use for, or rather an abuse, when she abruptly pushed me away. More precisely, she pushed me back with such ferocity that I lost my balance and stumbled backwards.

'And now leave me alone!' she said sternly.

Then she sat down on the bottom stair and in broken phrases, as in the early days, went on and on:

'Nobody could touch me, nobody…after that death…I felt sure…absolutely…so don't accuse me. I don't lie. But the world is corrupt and confusing, as Pascal thought. I am trying to remain good…choose only what is authentic, but things are formidably complex. And there is something else…call it voluntary surrender. You too may understand …what I can confess to you now…a total response…when the time comes…when the time has come.

'I am sorry, not personally but as a human being…for any joy bought with the pain of the other. And because I admit you were gentle, in your way. But this formidable complexity …everywhere, also hidden inside and between us…'

She lowered her voice and at the same time became less tense.

'And Ahmed…he is so simple in comparison. Perhaps he does not love me…he just makes love to me…without difficulty. We don't talk much, you know, certainly not about death…he forces me to be…different.'

She began to laugh. 'Ahmed, my young Arab, is so simple and…innocent. Perhaps thirty years younger than I, but I am not ashamed. Because simply to touch his skin is a joy, but he is also spiritual. We are both looking and searching… . And my late husband approves of him, resembles him when he too was young and fantastic.'

She laughed again quite wildly.

'And I won't let you rob me of my joy! It is metaphysical…it is, I feel…a rebirth. Yes, I can see now the marvellous cycle…birth, death and rebirth, birth, death and rebirth.' She paused as if waiting for an answer, then started to laugh again, quietly, to herself. 'Anyway that's what happened to me. At least I hope it was me.'

She stopped, turned round and started to climb the stairs. I can't remember saying goodnight or anything else. I hardly slept all night and when I woke – after nine o'clock, too late for breakfast – the phone in her room was dead. Minutes later the woman at the reception informed me that 'Madame' had checked out quite early, before eight o'clock, returning the key and taking her luggage. She added – quite uncalled for and indiscreetly, perhaps to make me feel guilty – that on departure Madame looked *très morne,* which to me suggested 'mournful'.

I want to add only that I felt nothing for her after that. I could neither blame nor praise. I had no further contact with Gisele, and I have no idea what happened to her, whether she ever recovered or not.

V

UNMARRIED

Waiting for someone is not my strong point; after a quarter of an hour my pulse beats faster and I tend to foresee disaster. On this occasion, when Pamela kept me waiting long after the appointed time – for afternoon tea in the perfectly designed Pump Room – I felt wrenchingly apprehensive. The Tompion clock struck half past four, and the place was due to close at five. The sound of the clock might have passed unnoticed in the middle of a conversation but it struck my solitude with the force of a hammer blow. Forty years of old waiting had somehow got sucked up and compressed into an hour or so of new waiting, reminding me of repeated postponements, with indefinite, merely potential meetings. Now a squad of unpleasant sensations culminated in a nervous anticipation of pain. Why wait for pain? I felt an urge to leave, run to the station and take a fast train back to London (I knew there was a First Great Western train every half hour).

Nevertheless, I managed to stop my worst thoughts as one might staunch a bleeding. The tried old method of self-control, thinking intently on some unrelated object, worked tolerably well on this occasion. First I tried to estimate the market value of that antique clock. Then I pondered the mechanism of the timepiece, the ingenious device that showed the difference between solar and mean time. I focused on mankind's progression from the sundial to the complexities of escapement and cogwheels, and so on to the digital clock of our restless age, showing the minutes and the seconds in red light in the darkness of my hotel room, at 4.32.03 for example, the unpredicted time for a piss. A general meditation on time wasted is to be avoided as that way madness lies.

Why did she let me down that time, in my hour of need? Bad timing. But it happened so long ago.

By-passing that thought, I chose to contemplate, out there, the Chippendale chairs – mere reproduction – decidedly preferring the plain to the ornate carving. One of the chandeliers hung more or less above my head – like pure icicles, or frozen waterfall, frozen time. Then I was disturbed by another wave of the same memory.

Shall I confront her with the past? She knew that I had been ill, that time, and must have known that her desertion risked my relapse.

One glance at the cream-coloured columns and the exquisite frieze restored my balance. A mazurka from the piano, and a high-pitched melody played on a flute drifting in from the street, completed the scene. Looking up, I could see through the tall Georgian windows an acrobat balancing on top of one small wheel, whirling three flaming torches and bowing to the applause. The tables, all covered in fine white cloth, were placed so far apart that hardly a word reached me from the conversation of couples at other tables – it would have been futile to try eavesdropping. Everywhere I saw couples with a sprinkling of children made to sit still by parents visibly in control. The hushed voices, as much as the commanding tone of reticence, suggested the survival of an antique, more polite society, so that I felt like a solitary time traveller re-visiting a supposedly vanished world. I had told myself that an amicable meeting in that meticulously chosen place might become the high point of the year. It might have been, if only Pamela had arrived on time, as arranged, to harmonise with my effort to create a blithe reunion. A reconciliation. I, for my part, had decided in advance to let bygones be bygones. We would simply confine ourselves to subdued feelings – all passion spent, the old saying – and polite conversation. I had even begun to rehearse the appropriate sayings and gestures for such a rendezvous. Looking out at those pacifying hills from the train, passing the great white horse at Westbury, I superimposed the gentle lineaments of her face on the gently rolling landscape.

But why was she so late? Was it not a deliberate trick to undermine me? Or an attempt to demonstrate that she, once again, couldn't care less? Some kind of moral insanity: she didn't want me to remember the twenty-year old girl, high-minded and loving, she preferred to hurl me back into betrayal and—

A persistent waiter interrupted my thoughts for the second time. So I ordered lemon tea with a croissant. The taste of the tea, Darjeeling, brought back memories of that time – in this place – with a sharpness that I could hardly bear. I suddenly knew that I had no choice but to confront her.

★

After you had left me, I ran through the streets like a long-distance runner, like a madman, ran round and round the Circus until nightfall, in the dark, down to the river where I stood above the Weir, ready to jump. Only one thought held me back – perhaps we could come together again, in a year or two or three, who cares how long if, in the end, you came again to show, not love, not kindness, no, just a faint flicker of light, to see a little less darkly. Since it was no longer possible to see in full light. All I needed was a clue or friendly guide. Why did you desert me? Out of the blue, like a slut. Out of sheer hysteria? Not as much as a hint, apart from a quick ref to that fool, when everybody knew he couldn't and wouldn't last, and you not the right type whatever else. Perhaps delayed teenage bewilderment, prolonged virginity, all those lofty ideas and too much church-going, solemnly quoting the Greek New Testament, certainly Greek to me. And all the time refusing a hug, let alone a kiss or the body thing, touching, even a handshake. Alone in your narrow bed in a shabby bedsitter, what were you thinking? Did you think that intellect was enough? No passion, nothing to show, reveal, express, as if hobbled or castrated, I nearly said, more politely sterilised or whatever the exact operation needed to extract... . Some fragments from an iceberg remain, floating off Greenland, which is not in the least green as every idiot knows. Why can you never come?

★

Shortly before closing time a woman came towards my table. The stranger stopped, hesitated and, as she stood there, I noticed that she had no waistline, only straight vertical body lines. My glimpse took in the aged head under an old-fashioned hairdo, greyish cheeks and pale lips puckered or, to be exact, resolutely clamped. An attempted smile only emphasized her heavy eyelids, an attempted welcoming look seemed menacing to me.

'Donald,' I heard a familiar-sounding voice weakened by time, 'I'm desperately sorry to be so late. There was a terrific jam on the M4, I don't know what caused it. I feel dreadfully sorry about this but, really, what could I do?'

I realised that she didn't have a mobile telephone, nor did I. Her excuse sounded genuine, I wanted to accept it –

and her – and I made an effort to overcome my double disappointment: the lateness compounded by her frightening appearance, at first sight at least. Then I tried to reconstruct her ruined face, to conjure up its pristine, undamaged beauty.

The Pump Room was ready to close and we had to leave almost at once. The pianist played a tune that sounded like the can-can, something from Offenbach, how grotesque. Then the music stopped, the waiters in their yellow and black waistcoats stood by idly. My disappointment deepened for, before those dark memories surfaced, I had chosen this place as a benign reminder to help my search for the past.

Outside it had started to rain, not exactly pouring but raining so persistently that the magnificent street scenery was polluted. A chill wind got under our umbrellas. It became impossible to saunter, to sit on a cafe terrace, or focus on some tempting shop windows full of antiques. The cheerful skaters on Queen Square had all gone. The smug couples pushing prams had vanished. Yet only half an hour earlier I had seen the place illuminated by the mellow light of the late afternoon, people were sitting around in the open air, chatting or watching the buskers and the immobilised men impersonating statues – midwinter spring. We lost that gift in a moment. The season had changed into something not at all remarkable, the middle of winter. But we persisted in walking on, under our umbrellas.

'So how are you?' she said more gently than I expected. But I wanted from her something less banal as an opening.

'I'm afraid all this waiting has given me a headache. Though it is not your fault, evidently,' I added as a softener.

'I'm sorry, again. But, really, how are you generally? Your short letter gave the impression that you were thriving.'

'That's because I was looking forward…'

'Ah, and now you have regrets?'

I was reminded of her quick intuitive responses and told myself to stop exhibiting traces of my resentment. But I could not stop, and I made a few other remarks that she immediately interpreted as offensive. In less than ten minutes we managed to reduce our meeting to a duel.

I kept a wary eye on the shop windows, my long-engrained professional habit, noting a mobile clutter-busting table with five drawers and two side racks that promised a 'tidy home' to magazines and newspapers. Meanwhile I confined my part of the conversation to pleasantries, on the whole. She said next to nothing about herself, no doubt in response to my poor start. A little later I tried but failed to deepen our communication. And then chance undid my best intentions again. Not far from the Theatre Royal we were passing a luxurious shop, its windows decked out in a variety of trailing white gowns, splendidly tailored, light in texture and design. Evidently a wedding dress outfitter, a bridal paradise, hardly relevant to time present. After all, both of us had remained unmarried; and we were well past the age when one might indulge in wishful thinking about nuptials or regrets for missed opportunities, et cetera. I don't know what possessed me when I stopped to gaze at those gowns and pointedly asked a silly question: 'So how do you feel about that ceremony now – after all those years?' Pamela made no answer and walked on quite briskly, so much so that I had difficulty keeping up with her. Then she slipped on the proverbial slippery pavement and had what looked like quite a bad fall. I rushed to help her up, and as I did so some of my more generous feelings returned and I again vowed to take care not to summon our demons. But Pamela did not thank me for lifting and steadying her, on the contrary. She started to cry and hurled one or two abusive remarks at me. They were indistinct but I seemed to hear her hiss at me, 'You are beastly!' The schoolgirl remark amused me instead of making me feel repentant. Then Pamela began to drag her feet, even limping slightly, and turned to walk silently towards the car park where she had left her car. I immediately realised that we were risking a bad ending and improvised an alternative: I invited her to early dinner. After some hesitation she accepted, probably influenced more by hunger – she had not eaten since breakfast, she had told me – than a genuine desire to restore our friendship, if that is the word.

★

We ended up in a French restaurant, I think Café Rouge, where both of us ordered identical food, *coq au vin,* and shared a bottle from Languedoc. I thought Pamela was beginning to enjoy herself, up to a point, and I was relieved. But suddenly she turned on me. I don't remember having said anything provocative on that occasion, she just became defensive on the spur of the moment.

'You are obviously trying to make me feel guilty,' she said sternly.

I expressed surprise and tried to divert her attention, but she went on accusing me of having let her down – she used a stronger word, what was it? – long before she had done anything to hurt my feelings. For a month or two, after our break, she had felt she couldn't go on, she had kept crying in public places and was unable to work. She had put my photograph out of sight and burned my letters. She had stayed with her mother for two long weekends, seeking consolation in vain, though she couldn't tell her, couldn't bring herself to confide in her, the misery and the shame.

'So you see, Donald, you brought your troubles on yourself.'

I was at a loss to find some substance in her general accusation and reminded her that I had said nothing.

'I don't just listen to what you say,' she said. 'I am aware of what you think, your whole stance. You want to blame it all on me.'

She was working herself up into fierce indignation. Slowly and obscurely she outlined a story of how I had 'dated' someone called Julia at the apex – apex? – of our relationship, an act of treachery. At that point I vaguely recalled 'going out' once only with a girl student. I never saw her again.

'She was interested in opera and so... . And, for heaven's

sake, that was forty years ago and you did not protest at the time. So why now?'

'Are you trying to lie to me only or to yourself too?'

I assured her that I was trying to tell the truth and I wondered how she managed to make mountains out of a tiny molehill like that.

'I can see it absolutely clearly now, and I can say it now. You thought that girl was more sexy.'

'We did not think like that in those days,' I said.

'You did. Under plain cover. Hypocrite.'

I reaffirmed that Julia – was that her name? – and I did have a shared interest in opera.

'And I wanted to protect you, Pamela, from excess closeness. We were so young and insecure, unqualified and poor. And it was a different age,' I added, 'utterly different. To get too close to a woman meant a full commitment…'

'Yes, an engagement to marry. And that's what you wanted to avoid. You wanted a good time with, excuse me, a whore. What a cliché, I'm sorry. Plus, your minimal attentiveness, plus, plus, plus, which all added up to minus,' she said with a passion I found astonishing, so late in the day.

I reminded her that we went on to have quite a good time ourselves for several months, seeing films, exhibitions and caves.

'Yes,' she said, 'and you abandoned me in Wookey Hole.'

'What?' I laughed, a little practical joke, obviously. 'You could admire the stalagmites and stalactites on your own.'

'Except that I was terrified. And I saw it as a gesture summing up the way you treated me.'

'Nonsense.'

'I saw it as a clairvoyant might see.'

'Yes, they see things that never were.'

And so our dialogue continued until I, for one, felt exhausted. It has been a wretched day that had turned into the opposite of what I had expected. And then, in a sudden flash, I made a new connection: clearly, Pamela had deserted me, in my greatest need, that time, as an act of revenge. Slowly and tactfully, at least trying to be tactful, I put it to her that she had been motivated by a desire to punish me. (Or would she really have jilted me for the sake of a twerp? I couldn't bring myself to ask.)

★

Towards the end of our dinner I clearly saw the need for us to part as soon as possible, without ceremony but also without rancour. Indeed I was looking for an opportunity to brighten our leave-taking. I looked for some grace. To that end I offered to accompany her to the car park before I caught a late train back to London. The rain had stopped but the streets were still wet and shiny with puddles reflecting coloured lights. On our way we stopped to admire the stonework of the Abbey, a parish church illuminated like the great cathedrals of Europe. I looked up at the sculpture, at the angels climbing up ladders – to reach heaven? – and noticed a headless angel, no doubt decapitated by Puritan iconoclasts. Why did that local instance of pointless mutilation disturb me so? I think I associated it with damaged lives and instantly started thinking of Pamela with more compassion than anger.

How did we find ourselves spending a night in the same hotel at the end of a painfully contested half day? The cause was almost laughably simple: two tyres of Pamela's car had got punctured by hooligans and it was too late to get them mended that night. We wasted time and, in the end, we realised that it was too late to travel in any comfort at all. After considering various permutations of an exit plan, both of us decided to check in at a reasonably good three-star hotel —of course in separate rooms. Nevertheless, I could tell from the manner of the receptionist that he had immediately assumed that we two were inseparable, the ultimate irony after more than forty years of separation.

I felt tired and I was inwardly determined to avoid further recrimination. I invited Pamela for a drink, just one glass of sherry in the hotel bar, so as to prepare for a peaceful exit, an eventless goodnight. Then I made a mistake: I praised her, with some emphasis, for having managed so well, all those years, on her own. Unwittingly I had evoked the very subject that I wanted to avoid; Pamela heard more than I might conceivably have wanted to say, and she retorted with increasingly savage indignation. First she asserted that she was undoubtedly better off without a male companion than with one, given the questionable quality of those men she had come to know, unluckily. Next, as if wanting to provoke me, after my silence, she insinuated that I – unlike herself – would not have stood the test of celibacy. Strange words.

'The trouble is you simply haven't got enough imagination about other people's lives, about my life. Because you belong to that ignorant mainstream horde of men who assume that a single woman must have a poor life, no life. But you should know that—' she lowered her voice as two men in the bar kept looking in our direction, smirking '—I had a full life. I had a career, I had friends, I had a good male friend, we went bell-ringing together for years. And I travelled to all sorts of places, bird-watching at the Danube delta. I learned to speak modern Greek, up to a point, I climbed half way up the Rocciamelone, when I was younger, and I coped with my diabetes. And what did you do?'

I continued my long silence and Pamela lowered her voice further, this time fraught with emotion.

'And I might have had children except that…'

'Except what?' I blurted out, trying to hide my curiosity. 'And how?' I added.

'How dare you…' Her voice trailed off disconsolately.

'Tell me.'

'Oh, what's the point? It's all so utterly, utterly futile.'

There was a deeper note in her voice, an undertone of tension, that vexed me more than all her previous negative remarks. On a sudden impulse I asked:

'So, through all those years, did you manage to preserve your virginity?'

Now it was Pamela's turn to be silent. Her eyes flashed in anger, quite a different look from her earlier, fairly benign looks of disapproval. Then she hung her head and just sat there silently. Finally she stood up slowly, picked up her handbag with a disciplined gesture, and walked out.

As soon as I had reached my room, I tried to get some sleep. Instead I entered an infinite-seeming, restless half-sleep, trying to unwind the day's events. I felt responsible, not guilty, for what had gone wrong and I started planning possible ways of making it good. How could I free both of us from our chained thoughts and feelings? The long, dark shadow of the past – our prison, hers and mine. 'The pity of it,' I kept repeating the familiar words. We had wasted each other when we might have used our gifts for mutual fulfilment.

I suddenly realised that I had been thinking *her* thoughts, as a solemn, even pious voice had crept into my mind. Once she used to quote all sorts of texts for 'pilgrim souls', no less, quoting even holy scripture on occasion, to counter despair, for example 'Blessed are the meek, for they shall inherit the earth.'

I must go to her at once then, the idea came to me without forethought. But it was unthinkable: how could I enter that room? The room of a woman who had been inaccessible even in our time of closeness or make-believe love, more than forty years ago. Now estranged beyond repair. Yet to prove that it was possible to care only for her, her being well...

I climbed out of bed, got half-dressed and walked down the dimly lit corridor to her room. I knocked, and knocked again but there was no reply. I had an impulse to open the door, perhaps force it open regardless, go to her, take her in my arms as never before, lie down beside her, with her, if only for a moment, say nothing at all, only try to transform – dispel the demon of obstruction. I tried the doorknob but the door was locked. Thinking that I could see a streak of light in the crack under the door, I crouched and peeped, but no, there was no sign of light coming through. Then I heard a sound I could not identify at first, muffled and spasmodic, a sound that reached me as an indistinct horror before I could formulate a name for it – sobbing.

★

I slouched back to my room with head bowed in a kind of reflex. I tried to get some sleep for the second time, in vain. My thoughts kept whirling in a constant blur. A noise reached me from a room in my corridor: a woman laughing, and almost crying through her laughter. Then a short silence and more of the same – a moaning cry. I recalled a hotel, somewhere in Brittany, where a printed notice was pinned above a double bed: 'cries of joy forbidden'. At any time such a sound would have been disturbing, but at that particular time – past one clock at night when I was struggling with my thoughts about Pamela – it was unbearable. I banged on the wall and soon all was quiet, probably in a spontaneous, exhausted silence that had nothing to do with my interference.

Not only was I unable to sleep, I felt a chill descend from head to feet though the room seemed quite well-heated and I was covered with blankets. A sense of waste dominated my thoughts again, a sense of wasted lives. Was not Pamela like a nun who could not enter an enclosed order? Wasted chastity. And my so-called relationships? They came in her wake: a curse, a waste of time, one after another 'a waste of spirit'. But what if I hadn't let her down first, all those years ago, and again today? Why did I fail to be generous? Ah, yes, her lateness and her miserable face opened the floodgates of the past. But can there be no forgiveness, only a chain of events and emotions? The manacles of the mind, someone said. Perhaps it never happened, or not like that, but time poisoned our story. And there is no present because it is blocked by the past. Astrophysicists say that we can see as far as the origin of the cosmos, the birth of stars fourteen billion years ago, but then, of course, we cannot see what those stars are like now. Their present condition is invisible, out of reach. We are light years away from each other. We cannot connect. I must wait for the morning and then – we shall go into a black hole, we shall never connect.

Towards the morning I felt colder still, I was shivering. Perhaps I had a fever. I had grown old that night. And our condition couldn't be changed or repaired. There is no compensation, no such thing as a second act in life. A streak of grey reached me through the curtains but the room got so oppressive that I wanted to leave at once.

★

Breakfast promised to be an ordeal. Pamela frightened me as she joined my table. She was wearing a thick, dark overcoat and a black hat half-covering her eyes, her skin looked grey. It was as if she wanted to emphasise 'the stranger' in every aspect of her being, whether consciously or not. I knew that she wanted to leave almost at once but I felt the need to make some sort of final bow, obeying some old-world courtesy. My dawn state got worse. No longer shivering, I felt numb in body and mind, I could observe and process my thoughts, in an agitated way, but I could feel nothing – except not feeling. As I had come down first, I had already brought coffee, juice and muesli to the table and, as soon as Pamela arrived, I offered to bring her whatever she wanted. But she refused everything, item by item. 'No,' came the answer, 'not now, no thanks, I'm not in the least hungry.' I was reluctant to start my little meal while she was just sitting there stiffly, hoping that perhaps she just needed time. So we sat there in awkward silence opposite each other by the square table that seemed to grow in size between us like something organic, some malignant growth.

I gazed idly at some of the pictures on the walls of the dining room: hunting scenes, Old England views and other rubbish. There was not one piece of furniture worth naming though that was hardly my concern at the time. I had no idea how to lighten the sense of desolation that had visited us. All that we had said yesterday inhibited further speech. From time to time I made some practical suggestion, offered to carry her luggage when collecting her car, paying her bill when paying mine (assuming that I was better off financially) and lightly sketched a possible trip to some place of interest, perhaps a place we had visited together in the past, like Stonehenge. I knew that my words had a hollow sound and were only uttered to fill the emptiness that engulfed us. I did not want to be the first to get up and leave and I resisted the temptation to break the silence; yet I also wanted to make a scene, break a glass, for example. (Years earlier Eveline did just such a thing, trying to provoke her husband in a public place, wanting blood rather than silent tension and misery.) The memory made me smile involuntarily, and Pamela noticed. She must have thought that the smile was directed at her, and she sat up, looking much more relaxed, and asked for a glass of orange juice. No, she did not ask but she did say 'yes' to my repeated offer. I pleaded with her, for the sake of her health if nothing else, and after a long pause she simply said, 'Yes.'

'Thank you for that word,' I said.

'Perhaps we'll meet again,' was her final response.

The word 'never' came to mind quite distinctly but I did not utter it. There was no question of pretending that we had a future but I could not end that particular present with any sense of finality.

Epilogue

I thought I could never begin again. They scolded me when I tried it last time, nagging me about the strain and the health risk, but tonight I feel I can try again, I must. So try I will, sorting all those papers for a few minutes, preserving a few pages but clearing out as much as possible in my old scribble. If I collapse before nightfall so be it, at least I shall have tried to re-arrange the chaos once more.

★

The task was beyond me, I might as well admit it. So I will continue to make preparations for the day...

What's wrong with dying anyway? I keep asking. I conclude that nothing is wrong with dying in itself, but the slowness of it, the clinging to the unfinished past, confuses the process. Only let go, let go of possessions and memories. It is a blessing to get more addled day by day. What little I still remember will soon be gone without a trace. No need for words to prompt images from the past.

A few patches of darkness remain, whatever I do at this late stage. Of course it would be simpler just to burn my false confessions, 515 pages on last counting. But it is too late for that. A friend has adamantly refused to return the top copy, muttering something about a small publisher who might be prepared to print it, someone just starting out, exploiting a niche in the market. Sheer folly.

The old saying 'all is vanity' covers just about everything I had ever done and written. Trying to fix the past is the final masquerade. And I regret everything. That's a fitter song for me than Piaf's long ago.

★

I came out of hospital sooner than expected. At first they must have thought that I was done for, but I am still here, feeding in my own stable. The diagnosis is uncertain. How can it be dementia, I ask, when I remember clearly what I can't remember? And I have no problem *at all* with 1066 or 1789, no more grandeur in furniture after the revolution, for example. I can do simple sums – addition, multiplication, long division – without the benefit of a pocket calculator; I can also remember the periodic table and the major rivers of Spain. It is just that I can't recall people, especially women, their names or their faces – both. Most of them have left behind nothing except a few scratches in the melting snow. Traces? Vestiges? I can hardly call them that. Meanwhile, I want to keep myself going, or staggering, without the burden of resentment.

Everybody is babbling about 'life is a dream' but such platitudes disturb my serenity. I happen to know perfectly well when I am awake and when I wake from another bad dream. I may look decrepit or barely conscious most of the time, but I can still repeat: 'This is not a dream.' And I know that the writing was not a dream; on the contrary, it was too material and therefore corrupt. Made of words.

In reality all those women are one.

When they come to me now, when I wake about half past four a.m., *they* all merge into each other. First they scatter and then they melt into one, the girl who embraced me, and the mature woman who betrayed me. The ice-age eyes of that old woman stare at me above nubile shoulders. All the faces get blurred, they dissolve at my slightest effort to identify any one. The first, the second and the third faces resemble the fourth, and the fifth, and so on, conjuring up buried faces in an infinite series. I see a female figure leaning between two mirrors and getting duplicated endlessly in a gallery of reflections. They are all leaning forward: head bent, high cheekbones, dark hair, radiant. I am for ever confronted with the same ambiguous gestures, summoning and enticing me in a moment of generous openness, then cancelling the gift in an instant. A voice, low-toned but rising in a foreign accent, then a cacophony of mocking voices. Then not even an echo from the hills across the lake. Now nobody calls and nobody returns my call, perhaps all the lines have been cut electronically. No more talking of birth, re-birth and death. No company for a meal, a walk, no climbing of towers that collapse.

I can remember hardly anything when I wake in a sweat,

for the second time, after five o'clock. Who was that dark-haired girl trying so hard to sleep with me before I woke? Such phenomena are impossible to identify, and exhausting too. Fortunately, my bed and my room are empty, that much could be verified by independent observers.

★

Today I saw the poplars beginning to shed their leaves.

Why not rest after that? 'Look at the poplars!' was all she said, all I could hear, as she lay in the grass by the towpath fully dressed.

I don't go out any longer. I could if I tried, for I have enough residual energy to walk a little and it might even be interesting to prove that I can still do it, but I don't feel the need for such an adventure. I have everything I need here, stored in the freezer and in my mind.

There is no difference between action and non-action, love returned or unrequited. Together for four years or four minutes or never, it is all the same. Travelling to Paris – or was it Mombasa or Puebla? – was pointless. I could have found better names for my marionettes perhaps, but the difference might be minimal. If Gisele is wrong, would Rosalyn or Priscilla be such an improvement? Or Helen – the name I found in a notebook: I wracked my brains trying to determine what I intended to do with her until it slowly dawned on me that she had dropped out of an Irish poet's line about Troy – nothing to do with me or my scribble. And I am tired of inventing names and faces or body shapes, an attitude or a style of conversation, a gesture, a posture, some idiotic impulse, and all the time note the gradual deterioration before the catastrophe.

★

Today I saw a poplar uprooted by the gale, the trunk broken as if by vandals. I saw it all from my window, my shelter, a secure place, a place of light and life, despite my thoughts.

It is said that Sophocles was delighted when in declining years he had lost all his desire for women. I concur. True virility lies in virtue.

Today I seem to feel better. I may go out after all, join a yoga class and get my torn shirt mended.

Today I seem to feel

★

Editor's Afterword

This manuscript came into my hands unexpectedly, in October 1999, after Donald Waterman's sudden death in a domestic accident. It is not clear to this day what motivated the author in choosing me to be his literary executor. For I did not know him well (the modest amount of information here disclosed had to be researched) as we tended to talk about impersonal things when we met. Once only did he cross a threshold of self-revelation, talking about his opinions, but not his life, over dinner in a London restaurant when in a tipsy state. Perhaps that encouraged DW to entrust me with the onerous task of storing his precious papers, the least I could do. No instructions came with the manuscript, neither for publication nor for pulping.

The manuscript itself was far from satisfactory: the format was inchoate and untidy, with almost fifty pages in hurried handwriting (a true manuscript) mixed with heavily corrected, haphazardly paginated and badly typed sheets of varying sizes, including some American and French writing paper possibly used during the travels related in two of the stories. A large number of small yellow Post-it notes had been inserted throughout the text, together with a few unrelated memoranda, telephone bills used as bookmarks, and the top of a pen serving as a paper clip. The original package was over five hundred pages long, unreadable without a sustained effort of reconstruction. All this struck one as anything but a pedantic product, coming from a man whose published work had been, as far as is known, confined to spare articles on antique furniture in a number of high quality trade journals. The whole thing looked like the work of a romantic student toiling away in ill-heated lodgings before the invention of the computer. The sheer number of spelling and/or typing errors was excessive by any standards, and we had to engage the services of an experienced proof-reader before the task of taming the text could be accomplished.

It took over a year to come to grips with the text and another year to give it a shape within comprehensible limits. Concerning the writer only two pieces of information emerged, possibly significant. One was that Donald Waterman had developed the awkward habit of punning, and accepting puns, on his own first name: his colleagues sometimes called him 'a bit of a Don'. His teasers could hardly have guessed that their light allusion to the adventures of Don Juan might lead to a mocking kind of role-playing in the memoir of an unadventurous man. The second piece of information was that, as a mature student, Waterman attended a creative writing seminar under the late Malcolm Bradbury at the University of East Anglia. He appeared on one occasion only, according to our informant, making a very slight impression. For his presence was inconspicuous: thin with thinning hair, aged about forty-five at the time of the seminar, soft-spoken with a hesitant manner, apparently not in the least inspired by a heated discussion on postmodern theories of narratology. We may, then, be dealing with a naive writer. If so, it is a naivety coupled with a self-consciousness that no tough contemporary writer would wish to display.

An editor, who in our time has to be something of a critic, must be aware of the complexities of any assumed first-person narrative. It is difficult, and sometimes impossible, to evaluate how far such a narrator is reliable or not, positioned somewhere between the polarities of the confessor and the impostor.

We cannot test the authenticity of the record against biographical evidence, as the material available is so scant; and what little we do know cannot be accurately matched with details in the tales. The reader must then remain the final judge of the text both aesthetically and ethically, unaided and unprejudiced.

There is little evidence to substantiate 'the inner story' of a quest for love and the continual loss of love, as it has proved impossible to trace living persons who might verify, or at least evaluate, some of the erotic episodes disclosed in the five tales. By contrast, 'the outer story' of travelling and *flânerie* was confirmed by two witnesses who did not, however, prove to be enlightening beyond a minimal testimony.

Born in 1935, Donald Waterman was seen by those who remembered him at all as 'a sad but smiling bachelor'. He lived alone in North West London for some thirty years. He had few if any close friends but a large number of professional acquaintances, more often women than men. He would frequently regale his companions with travellers' tales, tending to exaggerate his own part as a loser. He is said to have been quite good at mimicking accents and gestures, but was in danger of becoming a club bore through repetition, or variation on the theme. However, he was also a questioner and he knew how to elicit reminiscences from his interlocutor or interlocutress. One informant recalled a generally cautious rather than adventurous direction in his anecdotes.

There was no obituary. That in itself suggests a degree of obscurity, with professional activities limited to freelance advice on, and appraisal of, antique furniture, following just a few years of documented work for the West End firm of Marples and Paterson. His extensive travelling may well have been as much a hobby as a breadwinning necessity, partially funded from private means. It is rumoured that in his middle years he had been the recipient of a considerable legacy from a maiden aunt, which made affordable his predilection for prolonged residence in four-star hotels. From a sympathetic point of view, we might conjure up the image of a homeless wanderer in pursuit of moments of happiness or at least encounters; less sympathetically viewed, the writing itself points to a rootless fugitive whose life and loves resemble the futile experimentation of the amateur.

A comparable amateurishness marked his opinions, in so far as these can be distilled from the only serious conversation he once indulged in with the editor. At a time when anyone aspiring to a degree of intellectual distinction tends to theorise and problematise in the service of a dominant *ism*, Donald Waterman's stream of ideas rather suggested a man of leisure in pursuit of an aphorism. He would interrupt himself with asides, self-raised objections, quotations and qualifications. His arguments tended to be obsessive yet lightly satirical. While talking, he never looked one in the eye, a disconcerting habit, especially when combined with evasiveness. Had he advertised his writing project, he might have gained some attention. But there was no mention of such a project. Once he alluded to an 'inquiry' without specifying his topic. With hindsight, one may discern a hint of a subject in one of his fixed ideas, concerning the Albigensian heresy, the Cathars, also called the Church of Love – lamenting the evil that had crept into the world when Lucifer sent to men on earth a woman of dazzling beauty who inflamed them with desire. For that reason the Cathars refused to marry or if they did marry they would abstain from all sexual contact with a wife. Inevitably, their strict celibacy could swing into promiscuity. They lived a thoroughly dualistic life.

Was there not an underlying misogyny in that ancient heresy? When challenged, Waterman asserted that the Cathars ultimately put their trust in the counter-female, Sophia or wisdom, corresponding to Mary, redeemer of Eve, the pure feminine light, et cetera. He also refuted the teasing suggestion that he was a real antiquarian who lived in the past and cherished mythologies of the Madonna and the whore. He claimed to have befriended a radical feminist who got engaged in his ideas, which she called 'medievalism in a postpatriarchal scenario'. She encouraged him to elaborate the varieties of the noble and evil feminine types, which she saw as alternate phallic fantasies of repressed desire and transgression. However, there is no record of a sustained relationship or co-operation between the feminist and the fastidious adventurer.

If all this does not sound cogent, it must be said that Waterman's talk was far less so. In the course of our dinner he became flushed and animated and then dejected. With hindsight it is easy to see that he had been eager to tell us something that was beyond his power to tell within the frame of an otherwise ordinary conversation. By the end of the dinner he seemed unsteady, so much so that he collided with the glass door at the exit.